# 老人與海

The Old Man and the Sea

海明威 著
黃源深 譯

他是個老人，獨自駕了條小船，在墨西哥灣流捕魚。出海八十四天了，連一條魚都沒有到手。前四十天，還有個男孩跟著。可是一連四十天都沒捕到魚後，孩子的父母就說，這老頭真是晦氣，倒楣透頂[1]。孩子聽從吩咐，上了另一條船，第一個星期就捕到了三條好魚。看著老人天天空舟而歸，孩子心裡很難受。他常下岸去幫老人的忙，把成卷的釣線，或是手鉤、魚叉和纏在桅杆上的帆卸下船來。船帆用麵粉袋打過補丁，捲起來時，活像是常敗將軍的旗幟。

老人瘦骨嶙峋，頸背上刻著深深的皺紋，臉上留著良性皮膚腫瘤引起的褐色斑塊，那是陽光在熱帶洋面上的反射造成的。褐斑布滿了他的雙頰，雙手因為常常拽住釣線把大魚往上拉，鐫刻著很深的傷疤。不過，沒有一處傷疤是新的，每個傷疤都像無魚的沙漠裡風化了的沙土一樣古老。

1 原文為西班牙語。這個詞的正確拼法應為 salado，這裡省掉字母 d，疑是吞音所致。

He was an old man who fished alone in a skiff in the Gulf Stream and he had gone eighty-four days now without taking a fish. In the first forty days a boy had been with him. But after forty days without a fish the boy's parents had told him that the old man was now definitely and finally *salao*, which is the worst form of unlucky, and the boy had gone at their orders in another boat which caught three good fish the first week. It made the boy sad to see the old man come in each day with his skiff empty and he always went down to help him carry either the coiled lines or the gaff and harpoon and the sail that was furled around the mast. The sail was patched with flour sacks and, furled, it looked like the flag of permanent defeat.

The old man was thin and gaunt with deep wrinkles in the back of his neck. The brown blotches of the benevolent skin cancer the sun brings from its reflection on the tropic sea were on his cheeks. The blotches ran well down the sides of his face and his hands had the deep-creased scars from handling heavy fish on the cords. But none of these scars were fresh. They were as old as erosions in a fishless desert.

除了一雙眼睛，他渾身上下都很蒼老。那雙眼睛樂觀而且永不言敗，色彩跟大海一樣。

「聖地牙哥，」他們從泊船的地方爬上岸時，孩子對他說，「我又可以跟你去了，我們已經掙了些錢。」

老人教會了孩子捕魚，孩子很愛他。

「不，」老人說，「你在一條幸運船上，你可要待下去呀。」

「可是你記得吧，有一回你有八十七天都沒有捕到魚，可後來，一連三個星期，我們每天都捕到了大魚。」

「我記得，」老人說，「我知道你不是因為懷疑我不行才離開的。」

「是我爸讓我走的。我還是個小孩，總得聽他的。」

「這我知道，」老人說，「這很正常。」

「他不大有信心。」

Everything about him was old except his eyes and they were the same color as the sea and were cheerful and undefeated.

"Santiago," the boy said to him as they climbed the bank from where the skiff was hauled up. "I could go with you again. We've made some money."

The old man had taught the boy to fish and the boy loved him.

"No," the old man said. "You're with a lucky boat. Stay with them."

"But remember how you went eighty-seven days without fish and then we caught big ones every day for three weeks."

"I remember," the old man said. "I know you did not leave me because you doubted."

"It was papa made me leave. I am a boy and I must obey him."

"I know," the old man said. "It is quite normal."

"He hasn't much faith."

「是呀，」老人說，「不過我們有，是吧？」

「是的，」孩子說，「我在露臺飯館請你喝杯啤酒，然後我們再把這些東西拿回家去，好嗎？」

「幹麼不？」老人說，「兩個漁夫一起喝一杯。」

他們坐在露臺上。有很多漁夫取笑老人，老人卻並不生氣。那些年紀更長一些的漁夫瞧著他，心裡很難受，但他們沒有表露出來，只是客氣地談論著水流、釣線漂入水中的深度、一連的好天氣以及他們的見聞。那天收穫頗豐的漁夫已經回來了，他們把旗魚剖開，橫著鋪在兩塊木板上。板的兩頭各有一人抬著，踉踉蹌蹌朝魚庫走去。漁夫在魚庫那兒等待冷凍車過來，把魚運往哈瓦那市場。那些捕到鯊魚的人已經把魚運到海灣另一頭的鯊魚加工廠裡了，在那裡他們把鯊魚吊在滑輪上，取下魚肝，割去魚鰭，剝掉魚皮，把魚肉切成一條條的準備醃起來。

"No," the old man said. "But we have. Haven't we?"

"Yes," the boy said. "Can I offer you a beer on the Terrace and then we'll take the stuff home."

"Why not?" the old man said. "Between fishermen."

They sat on the Terrace and many of the fishermen made fun of the old man and he was not angry. Others, of the older fishermen, looked at him and were sad. But they did not show it and they spoke politely about the current and the depths they had drifted their lines at and the steady good weather and of what they had seen. The successful fishermen of that day were already in and had butchered their marlin out and carried them laid full length across two planks, with two men staggering at the end of each plank, to the fish house where they waited for the ice truck to carry them to the market in Havana. Those who had caught sharks had taken them to the shark factory on the other side of the cove where they were hoisted on a block and tackle, their livers removed, their fins cut off and their hides skinned out and their flesh cut into strips for salting.

一颳東風，一股魚腥味就會從鯊魚加工廠裡飄出來，飄過海港吹到這裡。但今天風轉為往北吹，後來風又漸漸地停了，所以只有一絲淡淡的腥味。露臺上灑滿陽光，很是愜意。

「聖地牙哥。」孩子喚道。

「嗯。」老人應道。他握著酒杯，回想多年以前的往事。

「我出去弄些沙丁魚來，讓你明天用，好不好？」

「不用了。玩你的棒球去吧。我還划得動，還有羅赫略可以幫忙撒網。」

「我想去。既然不能跟你去捕魚，那總該幫點忙吧。」

「你給我買了啤酒，」老人說，「你已經是個男子漢了。」

「你第一次帶我上船那會兒，我幾歲呀？」

「五歲，而且你差點就沒命了。當時我把一條魚拖上了船，那魚活蹦亂跳的，險些把船撞得粉碎。你還記得嗎？」

When the wind was in the east a smell came across the harbour from the shark factory; but today there was only the faint edge of the odour because the wind had backed into the north and then dropped off and it was pleasant and sunny on the Terrace.

"Santiago," the boy said.

"Yes," the old man said. He was holding his glass and thinking of many years ago.

"Can I go out to get sardines for you for tomorrow?"

"No. Go and play baseball. I can still row and Rogelio will throw the net."

"I would like to go. If I cannot fish with you, I would like to serve in some way."

"You bought me a beer," the old man said. "You are already a man."

"How old was I when you first took me in a boat?"

"Five and you nearly were killed when I brought the fish in too green and he nearly tore the boat to pieces. Can you remember?"

「我記得那魚尾巴使勁地拍打，撞斷了划手的坐板，還有你用棍子打魚的聲音。我還記得你把我推到船頭，那兒堆著一卷卷濕淋淋的釣線。我覺得整條船都在顫抖，我聽見你在用棍子打魚，就像砍樹一樣。我覺得渾身都是甜甜的血腥味。」

「你是真的記得，還是聽我說的？」

「從我們第一次一塊兒捕魚那會兒起，我什麼都記得。」

老人用他那雙被陽光灼燒過的自信而慈愛的眼睛打量著他。

「你要是我的孩子，我就會帶你出去冒冒險，」他說，「可是你是你爸媽的孩子，而且又在一條幸運船上。」

「我可以去弄些沙丁魚來嗎？我還知道上哪兒搞得到四個魚餌。」

「我今天還剩下一些魚餌呢，我把它們醃在盒子裡了。」

「我給你弄四個新鮮的來吧。」

"I can remember the tail slapping and banging and the thwart breaking and the noise of the clubbing. I can remember you throwing me into the bow where the wet coiled lines were and feeling the whole boat shiver and the noise of you clubbing him like chopping a tree down and the sweet blood smell all over me."

"Can you really remember that or did I just tell it to you?"

"I remember everything from when we first went together."

The old man looked at him with his sun-burned, confident loving eyes.

"If you were my boy I'd take you out and gamble," he said. "But you are your father's and your mother's and you are in a lucky boat."

"May I get the sardines? I know where I can get four baits too."

"I have mine left from today. I put them in salt in the box."

"Let me get four fresh ones."

「一個就好。」老人說。他從未失去希望和信心。而現在就好像微風拂過，他的希望和信心都被鼓舞起來了。

「兩個吧。」孩子說。

「那就兩個吧，」老人同意了，「不是偷來的吧？」

「我倒是想去偷，」孩子說，「不過，這幾個是我買來的。」

「謝謝你。」老人說。他太單純了，不會去想自己是什麼時候變得謙恭起來的。但他知道他已經變得謙恭了，還知道這並不丟臉，也沒有讓他喪失真正的自尊。

「看這水流，明天會是個好天。」他說。

「你要上哪兒？」孩子問。

「很遠的地方，等到風向轉了再回來。我想不等天亮就出海。」

"One," the old man said. His hope and his confidence had never gone. But now they were freshening as when the breeze rises.

"Two," the boy said.

"Two," the old man agreed. "You didn't steal them?"

"I would," the boy said. "But I bought these."

"Thank you," the old man said. He was too simple to wonder when he had attained humility. But he knew he had attained it and he knew it was not disgraceful and it carried no loss of true pride.

"Tomorrow is going to be a good day with this current," he said.

"Where are you going?" the boy asked.

"Far out to come in when the wind shifts. I want to be out before it is light. "

「我要設法讓船主在很遠的地方作業，」孩子說，「那樣，要是你捕到一個很大的傢伙，我們可以來幫忙。」

「他可不喜歡在太遠的地方捕魚。」

「這倒是，」孩子說，「但是我會看到一些他看不見的東西，譬如一隻鳥在捕魚，引誘他去遠海跟蹤鬼頭刀[2]。」

「他的眼睛有那麼糟糕嗎？」

「差不多全瞎了。」

「這倒怪了，」老人說，「他又沒有捕過海龜，那才是最傷眼睛的。」

「但你在莫斯基托海岸捕了好多年海龜，眼睛還照樣很好呢。」

「我是個怪老頭。」

2 原文 dolphin（海豚），實為當地人對鬼頭刀的稱呼。（編注）

"I'll try to get him to work far out," the boy said. "Then if you hook something truly big we can come to your aid."

"He does not like to work too far out."

"No," the boy said. "But I will see something that he cannot see such as a bird working and get him to come out after dolphin."

"Are his eyes that bad?"

"He is almost blind."

"It is strange," the old man said. "He never went turtle-ing. That is what kills the eyes."

"But you went turtle-ing for years off the Mosquito Coast and your eyes are good."

"I am a strange old man."

「你現在還有沒有力氣對付一條很大的魚？」

「我想還有。何況我還知道很多訣竅。」

「我們把這些東西搬回家去吧，」孩子說，「這樣我就可以去拿漁網捕沙丁魚了。」

他們從船上拿了一應器具。老人肩上扛著桅杆，孩子拿著木盒，木盒裡面裝有一卷卷編織緊密的褐色釣線，還有手鉤和帶柄的魚叉。船尾放著盛魚餌的盒子，旁邊有一根木棍，是用來制伏弄到船邊的大魚的。老人的這些家當沒有人會偷。但是船帆和沉重的釣線還是拿回家好，因為露水對這些東西有損害。儘管老人肯定當地人不會來偷，但他想，把手鉤和魚叉留在船上會是不必要的誘惑。

"But are you strong enough now for a truly big fish?"

"I think so. And there are many tricks."

"Let us take the stuff home," the boy said. "So I can get the cast net and go after the sardines."

They picked up the gear from the boat. The old man carried the mast on his shoulder and the boy carried the wooden box with the coiled, hard-braided brown lines, the gaff and the harpoon with its shaft. The box with the baits was under the stern of the skiff along with the club that was used to subdue the big fish when they were brought alongside. No one would steal from the old man but it was better to take the sail and the heavy lines home as the dew was bad for them and, though he was quite sure no local people would steal from him, the old man thought that a gaff and a harpoon were needless temptations to leave in a boat.

兩人一起順著路走到了老人的棚屋前，從開著的門進去。老人把裹著帆的桅杆靠在牆上，孩子在旁邊放下木盒和其他漁具。桅杆幾乎跟這個單間的棚屋一樣長。棚屋是用王棕——當地人稱作棕櫚[3]——的堅韌苞殼蓋成的。屋裡有一張床、一張桌子、一把椅子以及一方燒炭起火做飯的泥地。棕色的牆是用棕櫚結實的纖維質葉子砌成的，那葉子被壓得扁扁的，疊在一起。牆上有一幅彩色畫，是《耶穌聖心圖》，另一幅畫是《科伯聖母圖》，都是他妻子的遺物。本來，牆上還掛著一張妻子的著色照，但因為他一瞧見便想起自己形單影隻，就把它拿了下來，放在角落的一個架子上，一件乾淨襯衫底下。

「你吃什麼呀？」孩子問。

「一鍋黃米飯和魚。你想要吃一點嗎？」

3 原文為西班牙語。

They walked up the road together to the old man's shack and went in through its open door. The old man leaned the mast with its wrapped sail against the wall and the boy put the box and the other gear beside it. The mast was nearly as long as the one room of the shack. The shack was made of the tough budshields of the royal palm which are called *guano* and in it there was a bed, a table, one chair, and a place on the dirt floor to cook with charcoal. On the brown walls of the flattened, overlapping leaves of the sturdy fibered *guano* there was a picture in color of the Sacred Heart of Jesus and another of the Virgin of Cobre. These were relics of his wife. Once there had been a tinted photograph of his wife on the wall but he had taken it down because it made him too lonely to see it and it was on the shelf in the corner under his clean shirt.

"What do you have to eat?" the boy asked.

"A pot of yellow rice with fish. Do you want some?"

「不，我回家吃飯。要我幫忙生火嗎？」

「不用了。我等會兒自己來生火。或者我也許就吃冷飯了。」

「我可以把漁網拿走嗎？」

「當然嘍。」

漁網已經沒有了，孩子還記得是什麼時候賣掉的。不過，他們每天都要把這場戲演一遍。孩子也知道，那鍋黃米飯其實是沒有的，魚也沒有。

「八十五是個幸運的數字，」老人說，「你想不想看到我帶回來一條魚，去掉內臟淨重還超過一千磅？」

「我去拿漁網捕沙丁魚，你就坐在門口曬太陽好嗎？」

「好。我有一張昨天的報紙，可以看看有關棒球賽的新聞。」

孩子不知道「昨天的報紙」是否也是編造出來的。不過，老人從床底下取出了報紙。

"No. I will eat at home. Do you want me to make the fire?"

"No. I will make it later on. Or I may eat the rice cold."

"May I take the cast net?"

"Of course."

There was no cast net and the boy remembered when they had sold it. But they went through this fiction every day. There was no pot of yellow rice and fish and the boy knew this too.

"Eighty-five is a lucky number," the old man said. "How would you like to see me bring one in that dressed out over a thousand pounds?"

"I'll get the cast net and go for sardines. Will you sit in the sun in the doorway?"

"Yes. I have yesterday's paper and I will read the baseball."

The boy did not know whether yesterday's paper was a fiction too. But the old man brought it out from under the bed.

「佩里科在酒店[4]裡給我的。」他解釋說。

「我捕到沙丁魚就回來。把你的和我的放在一起，鎮上冰，明天早上分著用。等會兒我回來，你跟我說說棒球賽的消息。」

「洋基隊是不會輸的。」

「不過我擔心克利夫蘭印第安人隊會贏。」

「對洋基隊要有信心，孩子。想一想名將迪馬喬吧。」

「我怕底特律老虎隊和克利夫蘭印第安人隊。」

「小心點，要不然，你連辛辛那提紅人隊和芝加哥白襪隊都要害怕了。」

「你研究一下，等我回來告訴我。」

---

4 原文為西班牙語。

"Perico gave it to me at the *bodega*," he explained.

"I'll be back when I have the sardines. I'll keep yours and mine together on ice and we can share them in the morning. When I come back you can tell me about the baseball."

"The Yankees cannot lose."

"But I fear the Indians of Cleveland."

"Have faith in the Yankees my son. Think of the great DiMaggio."

"I fear both the Tigers of Detroit and the Indians of Cleveland."

"Be careful or you will fear even the Reds of Cincinnati and the White Sox of Chicago."

"You study it and tell me when I come back."

「你認為我們是不是該去買張彩券，末尾兩位數是八十五？明天是第八十五天。」

「可以是可以，」孩子說，「不過你那八十七天的偉大紀錄怎麼辦？」

「不可能有第二次了。你認為能搞得到末尾兩位數是八十五的彩券嗎？」

「我可以預訂一張。」

「一張要兩塊五。我們向誰能借到這筆錢呢？」

「這個簡單。兩塊五我總能借到手。」

「我覺得也許我也能。不過我盡量不借。一回借錢，二回要飯。」

「穿暖和些，老爺子，」孩子說，「別忘了現在是九月。」

「是大魚上鉤的月分，」老人說，「五月分人人都能捕到魚。」

"Do you think we should buy a terminal of the lottery with an eighty-five? Tomorrow is the eight-fifth day."

"We can do that," the boy said. "But what about the eighty-seven of your great record?"

"It could not happen twice. Do you think you can find an eighty-five?"

"I can order one."

"One sheet. That's two dollars and a half. Who can we borrow that from?"

"That's easy. I can always borrow two dollars and a half."

"I think perhaps I can too. But I try not to borrow. First you borrow. Then you beg."

"Keep warm old man," the boy said. "Remember we are in September."

"The month when the great fish come," the old man said. "Anyone can be a fisherman in May."

「現在我去捉沙丁魚了。」孩子說。

孩子回來的時候，老人在椅子上睡著了，太陽已經落下。孩子從床上拿來一條舊軍毯，鋪在椅背上，蓋住老人的肩膀。這肩膀不同尋常，雖然很老，卻依然有力。那脖子也仍然很壯實。老人睡著時，腦袋往前耷拉著，皺紋並不明顯。他的襯衫打過多次補丁，弄得很像船帆，經太陽一曬，褪成了深淺不一的顏色。不過，老人的頭很老，閉上眼睛時，臉上就沒有一絲生氣了。報紙攤在他的膝蓋上，有胳膊的重量壓著，才沒被晚風吹走。他赤著雙腳。

孩子走了，沒有驚動老人，回來時，老人還沒睡醒。

「醒一醒，老爺子。」孩子說，他伸手碰了一下老人的膝蓋。

"I go now for the sardines," the boy said.

When the boy came back the old man was asleep in the chair and the sun was down. The boy took the old army blanket off the bed and spread it over the back of the chair and over the old man's shoulders. They were strange shoulders, still powerful although very old, and the neck was still strong too and the creases did not show so much when the old man was asleep and his head fallen forward. His shirt had been patched so many times that it was like the sail and the patches were faded to many different shades by the sun. The old man's head was very old though and with his eyes closed there was no life in his face. The newspaper lay across his knees and the weight of his arm held it there in the evening breeze. He was barefooted.

The boy left him there and when he came back the old man was still asleep.

"Wake up old man," the boy said and put his hand on one of the old man's knees.

老人睜開了眼睛，一時彷彿從遙遠的地方回過神來。然後他笑了笑。

「你弄來什麼了？」他問。

「晚飯，」孩子說，「我們要吃晚飯了。」

「我還不是很餓。」

「來，吃飯。你不能光打魚不吃飯。」

「我倒是這麼幹過。」老人說著站了起來，拿起報紙，把它折好。然後開始疊毯子。

「把毯子圍在身上，」孩子說，「只要我還活著，就不讓你空著肚子去打魚。」

「那就活得長些，照顧好你自己。」老人說，「我們吃什麼呀？」

「黑豆燒米飯、油煎香蕉和一些燉菜。」

The old man opened his eyes and for a moment he was coming back from a long way away. Then he smiled.

"What have you got?" he asked.

"Supper," said the boy. "We're going to have supper."

"I'm not very hungry."

"Come on and eat. You can't fish and not eat."

"I have," the old man said getting up and taking the newspaper and folding it. Then he started to fold the blanket.

"Keep the blanket around you," the boy said. "You'll not fish without eating while I'm alive."

"Then live a long time and take care of yourself," the old man said. "What are we eating?"

"Black beans and rice, fried bananas, and some stew."

孩子從露臺飯館弄來了這些飯菜，用一個雙層金屬飯盒盛著。口袋裡放著兩副刀叉和勺子，每副都用餐巾紙包著。

「這是誰給你的？」

「馬丁，飯館老闆。」

「我得謝謝他。」

「我已經謝過了，」孩子說，「你就不用去謝了。」

「我要把一條大魚肚子上的肉給他，」老人說，「他這麼款待我們不止一次了吧？」

「我想是的。」

「那我要給他的就不只是魚肚子上的肉了。他很關照我們。」

「他還送了我們兩瓶啤酒。」

The boy had brought them in a two-decker metal container from the Terrace. The two sets of knives and forks and spoons were in his pocket with a paper napkin wrapped around each set.

"Who gave this to you?"

"Martin. The owner."

"I must thank him."

"I thanked him already," the boy said. "You don't need to thank him."

"I'll give him the belly meat of a big fish," the old man said. "Has he done this for us more than once?"

"I think so."

"I must give him something more than the belly meat then. He is very thoughtful for us."

"He sent two beers."

「我喜歡罐裝啤酒。」

「我知道。不過這是瓶裝的，哈圖伊牌啤酒。我得把瓶子送回去。」

「你真好，」老人說，「我們可以吃了嗎？」

「我在招呼你吃呢，」孩子輕聲說，「你沒有準備好我就不想打開飯盒。」

「現在我準備好了，」老人說，「我只要花點時間洗一下就行了。」

上哪兒去洗呢？孩子想。村子裡的供水站隔了兩條街，在路的另一頭。我得替他把水弄到這裡來，孩子想，還有肥皂和一塊像樣的毛巾。我為什麼那麼粗心呢？我得再給他弄一件襯衫、一件過冬的外套、一雙什麼樣的鞋子和另外一條毯子。

「你的燉菜好吃極了。」老人說。

"I like the beer in cans best."

"I know. But this is in bottles, Hatuey beer, and I take back the bottles."

"That's very kind of you," the old man said. "Should we eat?"

"I've been asking you to," the boy told him gently. "I have not wished to open the container until you were ready."

"I'm ready now," the old man said. "I only needed time to wash."

Where did you wash? the boy thought. The village water supply was two streets down the road. I must have water here for him, the boy thought, and soap and a good towel. Why am I so thoughtless? I must get him another shirt and a jacket for the winter and some sort of shoes and another blanket.

"Your stew is excellent," the old man said.

「你給我說說棒球賽的事吧。」孩子提出要求。

「我說過，在全美職業棒球聯賽中，就數洋基隊最厲害。」老人高興地說。

「今天他們輸了。」孩子告訴他。

「那不要緊。迪馬喬這個厲害的傢伙恢復了狀態。」

「他們隊裡還有其他人。」

「那是。但有他就不一樣了。在另一個聯賽中，布魯克林隊對陣費城隊，我肯定支持布魯克林隊。可我又想到了迪克．西斯勒，還有老公園[5]裡那些漂亮的擊球。」

「這種好球是再也見不著了。我見過的擊球數他打得最遠了。」

5 指費城的希貝公園，曾是費城棒球比賽的重要場地。

"Tell me about the baseball," the boy asked him.

"In the American League it is the Yankees as I said," the old man said happily.

"They lost today," the boy told him.

"That means nothing. The great DiMaggio is himself again."

"They have other men on the team."

"Naturally. But he makes the difference. In the other league, between Brooklyn and Philadelphia I must take Brooklyn. But then I think of Dick Sisler and those great drives in the old park."

"There was nothing ever like them. He hits the longest ball I have ever seen."

「你還記得過去他常來露臺飯館的時候嗎？我想帶他去打魚，但我膽子小，不敢開口。後來我讓你去說，可你膽子也小。」

「我知道。我們犯了個大錯，要不，他可能會跟我們去打魚的。那樣的話，我們會有一段終生難忘的回憶。」

「我想帶名將迪馬喬去打魚，」老人說，「據說他父親是個漁夫。也許他過去和我們一樣窮，能說得上話。」

「名將西斯勒的父親從來沒有過過苦日子。他——我是指他父親——像我這樣年紀的時候就在大聯盟裡打球了。」

「像你這樣年紀的時候，我在一條開往非洲的橫帆船上當普通水手，黃昏的時候我見過獅子在沙灘上出沒。」

「我知道。你跟我說過。」

「我們是談非洲，還是談棒球？」

"Do you remember when he used to come to the Terrace? I wanted to take him fishing but I was too timid to ask him. Then I asked you to ask him and you were too timid."

"I know. It was a great mistake. He might have gone with us. Then we would have that for all of our lives."

"I would like to take the great DiMaggio fishing," the old man said. "They say his father was a fisherman. Maybe he was as poor as we are and would understand."

"The great Sisler's father was never poor and he, the father, was playing in the Big Leagues when he was my age."

"When I was your age I was before the mast on a square rigged ship that ran to Africa and I have seen lions on the beaches in the evening."

"I know. You told me."

"Should we talk about Africa or about baseball?"

「我想還是談棒球吧，」孩子說，「跟我說說那個了不起的約翰．J．麥格勞。」他把J說成了霍塔。

「以前他有時候也到露臺飯館來的，但酒一下肚就很粗魯，說話嚴厲，不好相處。他的心思都放在賽馬和棒球上。至少口袋裡一直裝著馬的名單，電話裡動不動就提起馬的名字。」

「他是個能幹的球隊經理，」孩子說，「我爸爸認為他最能幹。」

「那是因為他上這兒來得最多，」老人說，「要是迪羅謝不間斷地年年都到這裡來，你爸會以為他是最能幹的經理。」

「說真的，誰是最能幹的經理，是盧克，還是邁克．岡薩雷斯？」

「我認為他們不相上下。」

「而最好的漁夫是你。」

「不。我知道還有更好的。」

"Baseball I think," the boy said. "Tell me about the great John J. McGraw." He said *Jota* for J.

"He used to come to the Terrace sometimes too in the older days. But he was rough and harsh-spoken and difficult when he was drinking. His mind was on horses as well as baseball. At least he carried lists of horses at all times in his pocket and frequently spoke the names of horses on the telephone."

"He was a great manager," the boy said. "My father thinks he was the greatest."

"Because he came here the most times," the old man said. "If Durocher had continued to come here each year your father would think him the greatest manager."

"Who is the greatest manager, really, Luque or Mike Gonzalez?"

"I think they are equal."

"And the best fisherman is you."

"No. I know others better."

「幹麼這麼說？[6]」孩子說，「好漁夫很多，有些非常棒。但你是獨一無二的。」

「謝謝。你讓我高興了。我希望別來一條太大的魚，證明我們都錯了。」

「要是你還是像你說的那樣健朗，就不會有能扳倒你的魚。」

「也許我並不像我想像的那樣健朗，」老人說，「但我掌握很多訣竅，而且我還有決心。」

「現在你該上床了，這樣明天早上你才會精力充沛。我會把這些東西送回露臺飯館去。」

「那麼晚安。早上我會叫醒你的。」

「你就是我的鬧鐘。」孩子說。

6 原文為西班牙語。

"*Qu va*," the boy said. "There are many good fishermen and some great ones. But there is only you."

"Thank you. You make me happy. I hope no fish will come along so great that he will prove us wrong."

"There is no such fish if you are still strong as you say."

"I may not be as strong as I think," the old man said. "But I know many tricks and I have resolution."

"You ought to go to bed now so that you will be fresh in the morning. I will take the things back to the Terrace."

"Good night then. I will wake you in the morning."

"You're my alarm clock," the boy said.

「年歲是我的鬧鐘，」老人說，「老人幹麼要醒得那麼早呢？是為了能度過更漫長的一天？」

「我不知道，」孩子說，「我只曉得年輕小夥子睡得香，起得晚。」

「我會記得的，」老人說，「我會按時叫醒你。」

「我不喜歡他來叫醒我，好像我不如他似的。」

「這我明白。」

「睡個好覺，老爺子。」

孩子出去了。兩人已經黑燈瞎火地吃了晚飯。老人脫了褲子，摸黑上了床。他把褲子捲起來做了個枕頭，把報紙塞進褲子裡，用毯子裹住自己，將餘下的舊報紙蓋住裸露出來的彈簧，自己就睡在報紙上。

"Age is my alarm clock," the old man said. "Why do old men wake so early? Is it to have one longer day?"

"I don't know," the boy said. "All I know is that young boys sleep late and hard."

"I can remember it," the old man said. "I'll waken you in time."

"I do not like for him to waken me. It is as though I were inferior."

"I know."

"Sleep well old man."

The boy went out. They had eaten with no light on the table and the old man took off his trousers and went to bed in the dark. He rolled his trousers up to make a pillow, putting the newspaper inside them. He rolled himself in the blanket and slept on the other old newspapers that covered the springs of the bed.

不一會兒他就睡著了，他夢見了孩提時代的非洲，長長的金沙灘和白沙灘，白得簡直刺眼，還夢見了高高的海岬和褐色的大山。如今他每晚都夢見生活在那片海岸上，在夢裡聽到海浪的咆哮，看到本地的小船破浪前進。睡夢中他聞到甲板上柏油和麻絮的味道，嗅著早上陸地微風帶來的非洲氣息。

平常他嗅到陸上的微風就會醒來，然後穿好衣服，去叫醒孩子。但今晚那風來得很早，睡夢中他知道時候還早，於是便繼續做夢，夢見島嶼的白色峰頂從海上升起，又夢見加納利群島形形色色的海港和錨地。

He was asleep in a short time and he dreamed of Africa when he was a boy and the long golden beaches and the white beaches, so white they hurt your eyes, and the high capes and the great brown mountains. He lived along that coast now every night and in his dreams he heard the surf roar and saw the native boats come riding through it. He smelled the tar and oakum of the deck as he slept and he smelled the smell of Africa that the land breeze brought at morning.

Usually when he smelled the land breeze he woke up and dressed to go and wake the boy. But tonight the smell of the land breeze came very early and he knew it was too early in his dream and went on dreaming to see the white peaks of the Islands rising from the sea and then he dreamed of the different harbours and roadsteads of the Canary Islands.

他不再夢見風暴，不再夢見女人，不再夢見轟動的大事，不再夢見大魚、打架、鬥力，也不再夢見妻子。他只夢見眼前的地方以及沙灘上的獅子。薄暮中，獅子們像小貓那樣在嬉戲，他喜愛它們，就像喜愛那個男孩一樣。他從未夢見過男孩。他就那麼醒來了，他從開著的門望出去，瞧著月亮，攤開褲子，穿在身上。他在棚屋外撒了尿，然後順著路走過去叫醒孩子。早晨的寒氣讓他直打哆嗦。但他知道，哆嗦會讓自己暖和起來，而且他馬上就要划船了。

孩子家的房門沒有上鎖。他推開了門，赤著腳悄悄地走了進去。孩子躺在外間的一張帆布床上，睡得很熟。此時，月亮正漸漸隱去，藉著灑進屋的月光，老人能把孩子看得一清二楚。他輕輕地拉住他的一隻腳握在手裡，直到孩子醒來，翻了個身看著他。老人點點頭，孩子從床邊的椅子上拿了褲子，坐在床上，穿了上去。

He no longer dreamed of storms, nor of women, nor of great occurrences, nor of great fish, nor fights, nor contests of strength, nor of his wife. He only dreamed of places now and of the lions on the beach. They played like young cats in the dusk and he loved them as he loved the boy. He never dreamed about the boy. He simply woke, looked out the open door at the moon and unrolled his trousers and put them on. He urinated outside the shack and then went up the road to wake the boy. He was shivering with the morning cold. But he knew he would shiver himself warm and that soon he would be rowing.

The door of the house where the boy lived was unlocked and he opened it and walked in quietly with his bare feet. The boy was asleep on a cot in the first room and the old man could see him clearly with the light that came in from the dying moon. He took hold of one foot gently and held it until the boy woke and turned and looked at him. The old man nodded and the boy took his trousers from the chair by the bed and, sitting on the bed, pulled them on.

老人走出門，孩子在後面跟著。他很睏，老人摟住他的肩膀說：「對不起。」

「幹麼這麼說？」孩子說，「男子漢就該這樣做。」

他們順著路朝老人的棚屋走去。黑暗中，一路上男人們扛著桅杆光著腳在走動。

兩人走到了老人的棚屋，孩子拿了放在籃子裡的幾卷釣線以及魚叉和手鉤；老人把裹著帆的桅杆扛在肩上。

「你想喝咖啡嗎？」孩子問。

「我們先把漁具放到船上，再去喝點咖啡。」

在一個清早供應漁人早餐的地方，他們用煉乳罐喝了咖啡。

「睡得怎麼樣，老爺子？」孩子問。要完全趕走睡意還是很難，但這時他已漸漸清醒過來了。

The old man went out the door and the boy came after him. He was sleepy and the old man put his arm across his shoulders and said, "I am sorry."

"*Qu va*," the boy said. "It is what a man must do."

They walked down the road to the old man's shack and all along the road, in the dark, barefoot men were moving, carrying the masts of their boats.

When they reached the old man's shack the boy took the rolls of line in the basket and the harpoon and gaff and the old man carried the mast with the furled sail on his shoulder.

"Do you want coffee?" the boy asked.

"We'll put the gear in the boat and then get some."

They had coffee from condensed milk cans at an early morning place that served fishermen.

"How did you sleep old man?" the boy asked. He was waking up now although it was still hard for him to leave his sleep.

「很好，曼諾林，」老人說，「今天我信心十足。」

「我也一樣，」孩子說，「現在，我得去拿你和我的沙丁魚，還有你的新鮮魚餌。我們的漁具都是他自己拿的，他從來不要別人拿。」

「我們不一樣，」老人說，「你才五歲我就讓你拿東西了。」

「我知道，」孩子說，「我馬上回來。再喝一杯吧，這兒我們可以賒賬。」

他走了，光著腳踩在珊瑚岩上，朝存放魚餌的冷庫走去。

老人慢悠悠地喝著咖啡。一整天他就吃這點東西，他明白應該喝下去。如今，他厭食已經好久了，而且他從來不帶午飯出海，船頭的一瓶水成了他一天唯一的需要。

孩子回來了，拿著沙丁魚和用報紙包著的魚餌。他們順著小路向小船走去，腳底觸碰著嵌著鵝卵石的沙灘。兩人抬起小船，讓它滑進水裡。

"Very well, Manolin," the old man said. "I feel confident today."

"So do I," the boy said. "Now I must get your sardines and mine and your fresh baits. He brings our gear himself. He never wants anyone to carry anything."

"We're different," the old man said. "I let you carry things when you were five years old."

"I know it," the boy said. "I'll be right back. Have another coffee. We have credit here."

He walked off, bare-footed on the coral rocks, to the ice house where the baits were stored.

The old man drank his coffee slowly. It was all he would have all day and he knew that he should take it. For a long time now eating had bored him and he never carried a lunch. He had a bottle of water in the bow of the skiff and that was all he needed for the day.

The boy was back now with the sardines and the two baits wrapped in a newspaper and they went down the trail to the skiff, feeling the pebbled sand under their feet, and lifted the skiff and slid her into the water.

「祝你好運，老爺子。」

「也祝你好運。」老人說。他把槳索繫在槳栓上，俯身向前，借著槳葉在水中的推力，在黑暗中把船划出港口。其他海灘上也有船隻出海，這個時候月亮已經落山，他雖然看不見它們，卻能聽見船槳入水和划動的聲音。

有時候個別船上會有人說話。但大多數船都是靜悄悄的，只有船槳入水的聲音。出了港口，船隻便四散開來，駛向有望捕到魚的那一片海域。老人知道他正向遠處划去，把陸地的氣息留在身後，划進清晨海洋的新鮮氣息裡。他划過一片水域，看到了水裡馬尾藻發出的磷光，漁夫管這個地方叫「大井」，因為在這裡海水突然深達七百英尋，水流衝擊海底峭壁，形成旋渦，因此彙集了各種魚類。在最深的海底洞穴裡，集中了蝦和餌魚，有時還有成群的槍烏賊，它們在夜間浮近海面，成為一切遊蕩著的魚的腹中之物。

"Good luck old man."

"Good luck," the old man said. He fitted the rope lashings of the oars onto the thole pins and, leaning forward against the thrust of the blades in the water, he began to row out of the harbour in the dark. There were other boats from the other beaches going out to sea and the old man heard the dip and push of their oars even though he could not see them now the moon was below the hills.

Sometimes someone would speak in a boat. But most of the boats were silent except for the dip of the oars. They spread apart after they were out of the mouth of the harbour and each one headed for the part of the ocean where he hoped to find fish. The old man knew he was going far out and he left the smell of the land behind and rowed out into the clean early morning smell of the ocean. He saw the phosphorescence of the Gulf weed in the water as he rowed over the part of the ocean that the fishermen called the great well because there was a sudden deep of seven hundred fathoms where all sorts of fish congregated because of the swirl the current made against the steep walls of the floor of the ocean. Here there were concentrations of shrimp and bait fish and sometimes schools of squid in the deepest holes and these rose close to the surface at night where all the wandering fish fed on them.

黑暗中，老人能感覺到早晨正在來臨。他划船的時候聽得見飛魚出水的抖動聲以及它們在黑暗中升空時直挺挺的魚鰭發出的嗞嗞聲。他很喜歡飛魚，因為在海洋上飛魚是他主要的朋友。他為鳥兒們感到難過，尤其是嬌小的黑燕鷗，它們總是在飛翔覓食，卻幾乎總是一無所獲。他想，鳥類中除了強盜鳥和壯實的鳥，生活都比我們艱難。為什麼海洋有時候那麼殘暴，鳥兒，譬如那些海燕，卻生得那麼纖巧？大海很仁慈，也很漂亮。但是大海也可能很殘暴，而且突如其來。這些鳥兒飛著，扎進海裡覓食，哀哀地小聲叫著，相比大海而言，這些鳥兒太脆弱了。

In the dark the old man could feel the morning coming and as he rowed he heard the trembling sound as flying fish left the water and the hissing that their stiff set wings made as they soared away in the darkness. He was very fond of flying fish as they were his principal friends on the ocean. He was sorry for the birds, especially the small delicate dark terns that were always flying and looking and almost never finding, and he thought, "The birds have a harder life than we do except for the robber birds and the heavy strong ones. Why did they make birds so delicate and fine as those sea swallows when the ocean can be so cruel? She is kind and very beautiful. But she can be so cruel and it comes so suddenly and such birds that fly, dipping and hunting, with their small sad voices are made too delicately for the sea."

他常常把大海想成 la mar[7]，那是人們喜愛大海時用的西班牙語稱呼。有時候，喜愛大海的人也說些大海的壞話，不過往往是把它當作女人來說的。一些年輕一點的漁夫，就是那些用浮標做釣線的浮子，出售鯊魚肝掙到大把錢，買了汽艇的人，把大海叫作男性化的 el mar，說成是競爭對手，或者是一個地方，甚或是一個敵人。不過老人總是把大海想像成女人，某種施予恩惠，或者不給恩惠的事物。大海要是做出什麼狂暴或者可惡的事情，那也是出於無奈。他想，月亮影響著大海，就像影響著女人一樣。

他從容地划著，並不覺得費力，因為很好地控制在他正常的速度之內。除了偶爾幾處水流的旋渦，海面一平如鏡。他讓水流替他完成三分之一的工作。天濛濛亮時，他發現自己比預期到達的地方要遠了。

7 西班牙語。mar 是「海洋」的意思，la 是前面的陰性定冠詞，下文的 el 是陽性定冠詞。

He always thought of the sea as *la mar* which is what people call her in Spanish when they love her. Sometimes those who love her say bad things of her but they are always said as though she were a woman. Some of the younger fishermen, those who used buoys as floats for their lines and had motorboats, bought when the shark livers had brought much money, spoke of her as *el mar* which is masculine. They spoke of her as a contestant or a place or even an enemy. But the old man always thought of her as feminine and as something that gave or withheld great favours, and if she did wild or wicked things it was because she could not help them. The moon affects her as it does a woman, he thought.

He was rowing steadily and it was no effort for him since he kept well within his speed and the surface of the ocean was flat except for the occasional swirls of the current. He was letting the current do a third of the work and as it started to be light he saw he was already further out than he had hoped to be at this hour.

我在「深井」打了一周的魚，卻一無所獲，他想。今天，我會找到狐鰹和長鰭鮪魚群，它們中間也許會有一條大魚。

天還沒有完全放光，他就放出了釣餌，讓船隨水流漂移。一個釣餌下到了四十英尋深的水裡；第二個是七十五英尋，第三、第四個進入藍色的海水，分別為一百英尋和一百二十五英尋深。釣餌用的是新鮮的沙丁魚，每個釣餌頭朝下，釣鉤的鉤身穿進餌身，都被紮好、縫結實了，釣鉤的所有突出部分，包括鉤彎和鉤尖，都裹在魚肉裡。釣鉤穿過每條沙丁魚的雙眼，在突出的鋼鉤上形成了半個環。大魚能碰到的鉤子的每一個部分，都是又香又好吃的。

I worked the deep wells for a week and did nothing, he thought. Today I'll work out where the schools of bonito and albacore are and maybe there will be a big one with them.

Before it was really light he had his baits out and was drifting with the current. One bait was down forty fathoms. The second was at seventy-five and the third and fourth were down in the blue water at one hundred and one hundred and twenty-five fathoms. Each bait hung head down with the shank of the hook inside the bait fish, tied and sewed solid and all the projecting part of the hook, the curve and the point, was covered with fresh sardines. Each sardine was hooked through both eyes so that they made a half garland on the projecting steel. There was no part of the hook that a great fish could feel which was not sweet smelling and good tasting.

孩子給的兩條新鮮的小鮪魚，或者叫長鰭鮪魚，都像鉛墜那樣掛在了兩條最深的釣線上。在其他釣線上，他用了一條大金鯵和一條黃狗魚。這兩個釣餌都已經用過，但仍然完好無缺，又用上好的沙丁魚增添了它們的香味和誘惑力。每根釣線都像大鉛筆那麼粗，纏在一根被侵蝕成綠色的釣竿上。這樣，魚一拖，或者一碰釣餌，釣竿就會下沉。每根釣線都有兩卷四十英尋長的釣線卷，必要時可以接到另外一卷備用釣線上，這樣，一條魚可以拖出去三百多英尋長的釣線。

此刻，老人一邊盯著船邊伸出的三根釣竿，看看有什麼動靜，一邊輕輕地划著小船，使釣線筆直地上下浮動，各自保持相應的深度。天已經大亮，太陽隨時都會升起。

The boy had given him two fresh small tunas, or albacores, which hung on the two deepest lines like plummets and, on the others, he had a big blue runner and a yellow jack that had been used before; but they were in good condition still and had the excellent sardines to give them scent and attractiveness. Each line, as thick around as a big pencil, was looped onto a green-sapped stick so that any pull or touch on the bait would make the stick dip and each line had two forty-fathom coils which could be made fast to the other spare coils so that, if it were necessary, a fish could take out over three hundred fathoms of line.

Now the man watched the dip of the three sticks over the side of the skiff and rowed gently to keep the lines straight up and down and at their proper depths. It was quite light and any moment now the sun would rise.

太陽淡淡地從海上升起。老人能看見其他船隻低低地貼近水面，橫切過水流散開，離海岸很近。隨後，太陽更亮了，耀眼的光照在水上。接著太陽升離了海面，平坦的大海將陽光反射到他的眼睛上，他的雙眼感到了刺痛。他沒有對著陽光划船，卻低頭往水裡瞧，盯著筆直伸進暗沉沉的水裡的釣線。他把釣線保持得比別人的都直，這樣，在黑暗的水流裡，每一個層面都有一個釣餌，在他所希望的確切位置上等待著游過來的魚。其他人往往讓釣線隨水流漂移，有時候釣線還在六十英尋深的水裡，漁民卻以為已深達一百英尋了。

不過，他想，我的釣線深度很精確，只不過是我不走運而已。可是誰知道呢？也許就在今天呢。每一天都是個嶄新的日子。走運固然不錯，不過我寧可保持精確。那樣，機會來臨時，你已經做好了準備。

現在，太陽已經升起來兩個小時，爬得更高了，朝東看已不再那麼刺眼。此刻，只能看得見三條船，它們顯得很低矮，遠在近岸的地方。

The sun rose thinly from the sea and the old man could see the other boats, low on the water and well in toward the shore, spread out across the current. Then the sun was brighter and the glare came on the water and then, as it rose clear, the flat sea sent it back at his eyes so that it hurt sharply and he rowed without looking into it. He looked down into the water and watched the lines that went straight down into the dark of the water. He kept them straighter than anyone did, so that at each level in the darkness of the stream there would be a bait waiting exactly where he wished it to be for any fish that swam there. Others let them drift with the current and sometimes they were at sixty fathoms when the fishermen thought they were at a hundred.

But, he thought, I keep them with precision. Only I have no luck any more. But who knows? Maybe today. Every day is a new day. It is better to be lucky. But I would rather be exact. Then when luck comes you are ready.

The sun was two hours higher now and it did not hurt his eyes so much to look into the east. There were only three boats in sight now and they showed very low and far inshore.

在我的一生之中，早晨的太陽總是很刺眼，他想。不過，我的眼睛還是好好的。傍晚，我可以直視夕陽而眼前不會發黑。傍晚的陽光也很強，但在早晨，太陽卻會刺痛眼睛。

就在這時，他看見一隻軍艦鳥展開長長的黑色翅膀，在他前面的上空盤旋。那鳥來了個急速俯衝，翅膀往後掠，斜著身子下來，隨後又開始盤旋。

「它看中了什麼，」老人大聲說，「不單單只是瞧、瞧。」

他緩慢而穩當地朝鳥兒盤桓的地方划去，划得並不急，保持著釣線上下筆直。但他已稍稍挨近海流，這是為了保持釣法正確，不過動作比他不利用這隻鳥時要快。

這隻鳥在空中飛得更高了，再次打著旋兒，翅膀紋絲不動。隨後它突然俯衝下來，老人看見飛魚躍出水，不顧一切地滑過水面。

All my life the early sun has hurt my eyes, he thought. Yet they are still good. In the evening I can look straight into it without getting the blackness. It has more force in the evening too. But in the morning it is painful.

Just then he saw a man-of-war bird with his long black wings circling in the sky ahead of him. He made a quick drop, slanting down on his back-swept wings, and then circled again.

"He's got something," the old man said aloud. "He's not just looking."

He rowed slowly and steadily toward where the bird was circling. He did not hurry and he kept his lines straight up and down. But he crowded the current a little so that he was still fishing correctly though faster than he would have fished if he was not trying to use the bird.

The bird went higher in the air and circled again, his wings motionless. Then he dove suddenly and the old man saw flying fish spurt out of the water and sail desperately over the surface.

「鬼頭刀，」老人大聲說，「大鬼頭刀。」

他收起船槳，從船頭下面取出一根細的釣線，線上有一截金屬接鉤繩和一個中號鉤。他裝上一條沙丁魚做魚餌，把釣線沿著船舷邊放下去，將另一頭繫在船尾帶環的螺栓上。接著他給另一根釣線也裝上了魚餌，釣線捲做一團被扔在了船頭的背陰處。他又划起船來，密切注視著那隻黑色的翅膀長長的鳥，此刻它正低低地在水面上覓食。

他正瞧著，卻見那鳥歪斜著翅膀又俯衝了下來，一邊跟蹤著飛魚，一邊瘋狂而徒勞地撲閃著翅膀。老人看見水面上有一個微微隆起的地方，那是大鬼頭刀追逐脫逃的飛魚時掀起來的。在飛魚的脫逃路線之下，鬼頭刀劃破海水，等飛魚一落下便飛快地扎進水裡。那是一大群鬼頭刀，他想。鬼頭刀散得很開，飛魚很難有機會逃脫。這鳥也沒有機會，因為飛魚太大，也太快了。

"Dolphin," the old man said aloud. "Big dolphin."

He shipped his oars and brought a small line from under the bow. It had a wire leader and a medium-sized hook and he baited it with one of the sardines. He let it go over the side and then made it fast to a ring bolt in the stern. Then he baited another line and left it coiled in the shade of the bow. He went back to rowing and to watching the long-winged black bird who was working, now, low over the water.

As he watched the bird dipped again slanting his wings for the dive and then swinging them wildly and ineffectually as he followed the flying fish. The old man could see the slight bulge in the water that the big dolphin raised as they followed the escaping fish. The dolphin were cutting through the water below the flight of the fish and would be in the water, driving at speed, when the fish dropped. It is a big school of dolphin, he thought. They are wide spread and the flying fish have little chance. The bird has no chance. The flying fish are too big for him and they go too fast.

他瞧著飛魚一再衝出水面，那隻鳥徒勞無功地行動著。鬼頭刀群已經離我而去，他想。它們游得太快、太遠了。但也許我會捉到一條離群的魚，也許我的大魚就在鬼頭刀附近。我的大魚一定在什麼地方呢。

這時，陸地上升起了山一般的雲，海岸成了一長條綠色的線，背後映襯著幾座灰藍色的小山。此時，海水已經變成了深藍色，深得幾乎發紫。他低頭往水裡瞧了瞧，看見深藍的海面上散布著紅色的浮游生物，也看到了此刻太陽射出的奇異之光。他留意讓釣線一根根筆直地下到水裡，進入看不見的深處。見到那麼多浮游生物，他很高興，這說明有魚情。這時，太陽升得更高了，在水裡變幻出奇異的光，這意味著天氣會很好。陸地上雲彩的形狀同樣說明這是個好天。但這時，那鳥幾乎看不見了，水面上什麼也沒有，只有幾塊黃色的馬尾藻，被太陽曬得褪了色，還有一個僧帽水母的膠質泡囊，紫顏色，有模有樣，閃出彩虹色的光，貼著船浮在水面上。那水母側向一邊，然後又豎直了，氣泡似的開心地漂浮著，身後拖著長長的紫色致命觸鬚，足有一碼長。

He watched the flying fish burst out again and again and the ineffectual movements of the bird. That school has gotten away from me, he thought. They are moving out too fast and too far. But perhaps I will pick up a stray and perhaps my big fish is around them. My big fish must be somewhere.

The clouds over the land now rose like mountains and the coast was only a long green line with the gray blue hills behind it. The water was a dark blue now, so dark that it was almost purple. As he looked down into it he saw the red sifting of the plankton in the dark water and the strange light the sun made now. He watched his lines to see them go straight down out of sight into the water and he was happy to see so much plankton because it meant fish. The strange light the sun made in the water, now that the sun was higher, meant good weather and so did the shape of the clouds over the land. But the bird was almost out of sight now and nothing showed on the surface of the water but some patches of yellow, sun-bleached Sargasso weed and the purple, formalized, iridescent, gelatinous bladder of a Portuguese man-of-war floating close beside the boat. It turned on its side and then righted itself. It floated cheerfully as a bubble with its long deadly purple filaments trailing a yard behind it in the water.

「水母[8]，」老人說，「你這婊子。」

他從輕輕划槳的地方往水裡望去，看見小魚像拖著的觸鬚那樣的顏色，它們游動在觸鬚之間和泡囊漂浮時所投下的小小陰影裡。小魚不懼毒性，但人可不行，有的觸鬚會纏住釣線，紫色的觸鬚纏在上面像黏泥一般。老人把魚拉上來的時候，胳膊上和手上會留下疤痕和傷痛，像是被有毒的藤蔓或橡樹刺傷那樣。不過水母的毒性發作很快，人痛得像挨了鞭子似的。

彩虹色的泡囊很漂亮。但它們是海洋裡最虛假的東西，老人愛看大海龜把它們吃掉。海龜見了它們，就從正面直逼上去，然後閉上眼睛，這樣通體都有硬殼護身，再把觸鬚之類一股腦兒吞下。老人愛看海龜吃掉它們，暴風雨之後他也喜歡在沙灘上從它們身上踏過，他長了繭的腳踩在上面，啪啪地響，他愛聽那聲音。

8 原文為西班牙語。

"*Agua mala*," the man said. "You whore."

From where he swung lightly against his oars he looked down into the water and saw the tiny fish that were coloured like the trailing filaments and swam between them and under the small shade the bubble made as it drifted. They were immune to its poison. But men were not and when some of the filaments would catch on a line and rest there slimy and purple while the old man was working a fish, he would have welts and sores on his arms and hands of the sort that poison ivy or poison oak can give. But these poisonings from the *agua mala* came quickly and struck like a whiplash.

The iridescent bubbles were beautiful. But they were the falsest thing in the sea and the old man loved to see the big sea turtles eating them. The turtles saw them, approached them from the front, then shut their eyes so they were completely carapaced and ate them filaments and all. The old man loved to see the turtles eat them and he loved to walk on them on the beach after a storm and hear them pop when he stepped on them with the horny soles of his feet.

他喜歡綠蠵龜和玳瑁，它們姿態優雅，速度快，價值高。他瞧不起又大又笨的赤蠵龜，但對它們並沒有惡意。赤蠵龜的龜殼黃黃的，做愛方式怪異，閉著眼睛愉快地吞吃僧帽水母。

雖然他乘船捕龜多年，對海龜卻並沒有什麼神祕主義的想法。他為所有海龜感到傷心，甚至包括像小船那麼長，有一噸重的棱皮龜。大多數人對海龜很殘酷，海龜就是被宰殺剁成了塊，幾個小時後心臟仍會跳動。不過老人想，我也有一顆這樣的心臟，我的手腳也跟它們的一樣。老人吃白色的龜蛋，讓自己長力氣。五月裡他從月初吃到月末，這樣九、十月分身子骨就會很結實，可以對付很大的魚了。

他每天還從一個棚屋的大桶裡舀一杯鯊魚肝油喝下去，那棚屋是很多漁夫用來存放漁具的地方。魚油放在屋裡，誰要喝就喝。多數漁夫討厭那味兒，不過這要比起大早好受，更何況還可以有效預防傷風流感，對眼睛也有好處。

He loved green turtles and hawks-bills with their elegance and speed and their great value and he had a friendly contempt for the huge, stupid loggerheads, yellow in their armour-plating, strange in their love-making, and happily eating the Portuguese men-of-war with their eyes shut.

He had no mysticism about turtles although he had gone in turtle boats for many years. He was sorry for them all, even the great trunk backs that were as long as the skiff and weighed a ton. Most people are heartless about turtles because a turtle's heart will beat for hours after he has been cut up and butchered. But the old man thought, I have such a heart too and my feet and hands are like theirs. He ate the white eggs to give himself strength. He ate them all through May to be strong in September and October for the truly big fish.

He also drank a cup of shark liver oil each day from the big drum in the shack where many of the fishermen kept their gear. It was there for all fishermen who wanted it. Most fishermen hated the taste. But it was no worse than getting up at the hours that they rose and it was very good against all colds and grippes and it was good for the eyes.

這時老人抬起頭來，瞧見那鳥又在盤旋了。

「它找到魚了。」老人大聲說。但不見飛魚衝出水面，也不見餌魚四散奔逃。不過老人正瞧著的時候，一條小鮪魚躍向空中，轉了個身，頭朝下落進水裡。陽光下，鮪魚銀光閃閃。一條魚才回身入水，另一條就跳了起來，四面八方都有魚在跳，它們攪動著海水，跳得很遠去追逐餌魚。它們驅趕著餌魚，圍著它打轉。

要不是它們游得那麼快，我會衝到魚群裡面去，老人想。他看著魚群攪出了白色的水花，還有那隻鳥此時正俯衝下來，闖入餌魚群。驚慌中，魚群被迫游向水面。

Now the old man looked up and saw that the bird was circling again.

"He's found fish," he said aloud. No flying fish broke the surface and there was no scattering of bait fish. But as the old man watched, a small tuna rose in the air, turned and dropped head first into the water. The tuna shone silver in the sun and after he had dropped back into the water another and another rose and they were jumping in all directions, churning the water and leaping in long jumps after the bait. They were circling it and driving it.

If they don't travel too fast I will get into them, the old man thought, and he watched the school working the water white and the bird now dropping and dipping into the bait fish that were forced to the surface in their panic.

「這鳥幫了大忙。」老人說。就在這時，船尾踩在他腳下的一圈釣線繃緊了。他放下槳，緊握釣線，開始往船裡拉，只覺得小鮪魚一抖一抖地拖著，愈往裡拉，魚抖動得就愈厲害。他還沒有把魚掄過船沿，扔到船裡，就已經看到水裡藍色的魚背和金色的兩側了。太陽下，那條魚躺在船尾，形如子彈，十分結實，瞪著大而愚蠢的眼睛，尾巴利索地快速抖動著，劈哩啪啦往船殼外板上撞死了。老人出於善意，在魚頭上敲了一記，又踢了它一腳。在船尾的背陰處，那魚的身子還在顫抖著。

「長鰭鮪魚，」他大聲說，「做釣餌倒不錯，總有十磅重吧。」

"The bird is a great help," the old man said. Just then the stern line came taut under his foot, where he had kept a loop of the line, and he dropped his oars and felt the weight of the small tuna's shivering pull as he held the line firm and commenced to haul it in. The shivering increased as he pulled in and he could see the blue back of the fish in the water and the gold of his sides before he swung him over the side and into the boat. He lay in the stern in the sun, compact and bullet shaped, his big, unintelligent eyes staring as he thumped his life out against the planking of the boat with the quick shivering strokes of his neat, fast-moving tail. The old man hit him on the head for kindness and kicked him, his body still shuddering, under the shade of the stern.

"Albacore," he said aloud. "He'll make a beautiful bait. He'll weigh ten pounds."

他記不得一個人獨處的時候是何時開始大聲說話的。以前他獨個兒時曾唱過歌，在小帆船或者捕龜船裡，獨自值班掌舵時曾在夜裡唱過。那孩子離開後只剩下他一個人時，可能是這時候他開始了大聲說話。可是他不記得了。他和孩子一起捕魚時，通常只在必要時才開口。晚上或者天氣惡劣為暴風雨所困的時候，他們會交談。在海上，沒有必要就不互相交談被認為是一種美德，老人向來這麼看，並加以推崇。可是現在既然不會打擾到別人，他便多次開口說出了自己的想法。

「別人要是聽見我在大聲說話，會以為我瘋了，」他大聲說，「不過既然我沒有瘋，我也就不在乎了。有錢人在船裡有收音機和他們說話，還給他們傳來棒球賽的消息。」

He did not remember when he had first started to talk aloud when he was by himself. He had sung when he was by himself in the old days and he had sung at night sometimes when he was alone steering on his watch in the smacks or in the turtle boats. He had probably started to talk aloud, when alone, when the boy had left. But he did not remember. When he and the boy fished together they usually spoke only when it was necessary. They talked at night or when they were storm-bound by bad weather. It was considered a virtue not to talk unnecessarily at sea and the old man had always considered it so and respected it. But now he said his thoughts aloud many times since there was no one that they could annoy.

"If the others heard me talking out loud they would think that I am crazy,"he said aloud."But since I am not crazy, I do not care. And the rich have radios to talk to them in their boats and to bring them the baseball."

現在不是想棒球賽的時候，他想。現在該想的只有一件事，那就是我生來要幹的事。在那個魚群附近，也許有一條大魚，他想。我只不過在吃食的長鰭鮪魚中捉到了一條離群的魚。魚群卻在遠方捕食，而且動作迅速。今天，海上出現的一切都游得很快，而且朝東北方向。難道這會兒就該是這樣嗎？或者，這是某種天氣的徵兆，只是我不知道而已？

此刻，他看不到綠色的海岸，只能看到藍色山巒的山頂，山頂看上去白白的，彷彿覆蓋著白雪，他還能看見雲彩，雲彩像是上空高高的雪山。海水深暗，陽光在水裡形成了折光。無數斑斑點點的浮游生物在高高升起的太陽的照射下已不見蹤影。藍色的海水裡，老人能看到的只有深深的大折光以及他那筆直地伸到水下一英里深的釣線。

鮪魚再次下沉。漁夫把那一類魚統稱為鮪魚，只有在出售時，或者用來交換做魚餌時才用適當的名稱來區分。這時陽光熱了起來，老人的頸背感受到了熱力，划著船便覺得汗水從背上直淌下來。

Now is no time to think of baseball, he thought. Now is the time to think of only one thing. That which I was born for. There might be a big one around that school, he thought. I picked up only a straggler from the albacore that were feeding. But they are working far out and fast. Everything that shows on the surface today travels very fast and to the north-east. Can that be the time of day? Or is it some sign of weather that I do not know?

He could not see the green of the shore now but only the tops of the blue hills that showed white as though they were snow-capped and the clouds that looked like high snow mountains above them. The sea was very dark and the light made prisms in the water. The myriad flecks of the plankton were annulled now by the high sun and it was only the great deep prisms in the blue water that the old man saw now with his lines going straight down into the water that was a mile deep.

The tuna, the fishermen called all the fish of that species tuna and only distinguished among them by their proper names when they came to sell them or to trade them for baits, were down again. The sun was hot now and the old man felt it on the back of his neck and felt the sweat trickle down his back as he rowed.

我可以讓船這麼漂著，他想，先睡一覺，將釣線的繩套纏在腳趾上，有什麼情況就會把我弄醒。可是今天已經是第八十五天了，我得好好用來釣魚。

就在他注視著釣線的當兒，伸出海面的綠色釣竿猛地往下一沉。

「很好，」他說，「很好。」他把槳收進船內，半點也沒有撞著船。他伸手去拉釣線，把釣線輕輕地夾在右手大拇指和食指之間，既沒有感到釣線繃緊，也沒有覺出有什麼重量。於是他輕輕地抓住釣線。不一會兒釣線又往下一沉，這回是試探性的一拖，虛晃一槍，沒有什麼重量。他很清楚這是怎麼回事。一百英尋深的水下，一條旗魚正在咬餌，手工製的釣鉤刺穿小鮪魚的頭部，露出的鉤尖和鉤身都被沙丁魚包裹著。

老人輕巧地抓住釣線，用左手把釣線從竿上解下來。現在他可以讓釣線穿過指間而不讓魚有拉緊的感覺。

I could just drift, he thought, and sleep and put a bight of line around my toe to wake me. But today is eighty-five days and I should fish the day well.

Just then, watching his lines, he saw one of the projecting green sticks dip sharply.

"Yes," he said. "Yes," and shipped his oars without bumping the boat. He reached out for the line and held it softly between the thumb and forefinger of his right hand. He felt no strain nor weight and he held the line lightly. Then it came again. This time it was a tentative pull, not soild nor heavy, and he knew exactly what it was. One hundred fathoms down a marlin was eating the sardines that covered the point and the shank of the hook where the hand-forged hook projected from the head of the small tuna.

The old man held the line delicately, and softly, with his left hand, unleashed it from the stick. Now he could let it run through his fingers without the fish feeling any tension.

在這麼遠的地方，這一定是本月裡的一條大魚，他想。吃吧，魚兒呀。吃吧。請吃吧。餌料是多麼新鮮，而你卻在六百英尺深的冰冷黑暗水底。在黑暗中再轉身回來，回來吃魚餌吧。

老人覺得釣線輕輕地拖了一下，接著又是一下，只是重了一些，準是沙丁魚的魚頭很難從鉤子上咬下來。隨後便沒有動靜了。

「來呀，」老人大聲說，「再轉身回來，聞一聞，魚餌不是很香嗎？趁新鮮吃吧，還有鮪魚呢。又硬、又涼、又好吃。別害羞，魚兒，吃吧。」

他等待著，釣線夾在大拇指和食指之間，眼睛同時盯著它和其他的釣線，因為魚很可能已經游上來或者游下去了。隨後，釣線又同樣地被輕輕拖了一下。

「它會吃餌的，」老人大聲說，「求上帝幫忙讓它吃吧。」

可是魚兒沒有咬鉤，它游走了。老人手裡什麼也感覺不到了。

This far out, he must be huge in this month, he thought. Eat them, fish. Eat them. Please eat them. How fresh they are and you down there six hundred feet in that cold water in the dark. Make another turn in the dark and come back and eat them.

He felt the light delicate pulling and then a harder pull when a sardine's head must have been more difficult to break from the hook. Then there was nothing.

"Come on," the old man said aloud. "Make another turn. Just smell them. Aren't they lovely? Eat them good now and then there is the tuna. Hard and cold and lovely. Don't be shy, fish. Eat them."

He waited with the line between his thumb and his finger, watching it and the other lines at the same time for the fish might have swum up or down. Then came the same delicate pulling touch again.

"He'll take it," the old man said aloud. "God help him to take it."

He did not take it though. He was gone and the old man felt nothing.

「它不可能游走的，」他說，「基督知道它是不會游走的。它正在轉身回來。也許它以前上過鉤，記憶猶新呢。」

接著他就感覺到釣線輕輕地動了一下，心裡高興起來。

「它剛才不過是在轉身，」他說，「它會咬鉤的。」

他覺出釣線輕輕地拖了一下，心裡高興起來。接著，他覺得釣線動得厲害，而且重得叫人難以相信，那是魚的重量。於是他讓釣線往下溜去，往下，再往下，放出了兩卷備用線中的一卷。釣線輕輕地滑過手指往水下去的時候，老人仍能覺出巨大的重量，儘管拇指和食指之間幾乎感覺不到什麼拉力。

「多大的魚呀，」他說，「這會兒正把魚餌咬在嘴邊，帶著它走呢。」

"He can't have gone," he said. "Christ knows he can't have gone. He's making a turn. Maybe he has been hooked before and he remembers something of it."

Then he felt the gentle touch on the line and he was happy.

"It was only his turn," he said. "He'll take it."

He was happy feeling the gentle pulling and then he felt something hard and unbelievably heavy. It was the weight of the fish and he let the line slip down, down, down, unrolling off the first of the two reserve coils. As it went down, slipping lightly through the old man's fingers, he still could feel the great weight, though the pressure of his thumb and finger were almost imperceptible.

"What a fish," he said. "He has it sideways in his mouth now and he is moving off with it."

然後它會轉身，把魚餌吞下去，他想。他並沒有說出口，因為他知道，好事一出口就不一定會來了。他知道這是一條很大的魚。他想像著這條魚橫叼著鮪魚，在黑暗中游走。就在這個時候，他感到魚不動了，但重量還在。接著重量增加了，他又放出一些線去。他一時加大了拇指和食指之間的拉力，釣線上的重量增加了，一直傳遞到水裡。

「它已經咬鉤了，」他說，「那我要讓它吃個夠。」

他讓釣線從指間滑下去，一面向下伸出左手，把兩卷備用線的一頭繫在另外一條釣線的兩卷備用線的環扣上。現在，一切已準備就緒。這時除了正用著的線圈，他還剩三卷四十英尋長的備用釣線。

「再吃一點兒吧，」他說，「好好吃。」

吃吧，鉤尖會刺進你的心臟，殺死你，他想。慢慢上來吧，讓我把魚叉刺進你的身體。行呀，你準備好了嗎？你吃夠了嗎？

Then he will turn and swallow it, he thought. He did not say that because he knew that if you said a good thing it might not happen. He knew what a huge fish this was and he thought of him moving away in the darkness with the tuna held crosswise in his mouth. At that moment he felt him stop moving but the weight was still there. Then the weight increased and he gave more line. He tightened the pressure of his thumb and finger for a moment and the weight increased and was going straight down.

"He's taken it," he said. "Now I'll let him eat it well."

He let the line slip through his fingers while he reached down with his left hand and made fast the free end of the two reserve coils to the loop of the two reserve coils of the next line. Now he was ready. He had three forty-fathom coils of line in reserve now, as well as the coil he was using.

"Eat it a little more," he said. "Eat it well."

Eat it so that the point of the hook goes into your heart and kills you, he thought. Come up easy and let me put the harpoon into you. All right. Are you ready? Have you been long enough at table?

「好吧！」他大聲說著，雙手猛拉釣線，收回了一碼，隨之又一次次使勁往回拉，雙臂輪番揮動，以身體重量做支撐，使出胳膊的全部力氣把釣線往回拉。

但毫無結果。魚一味地慢慢往外游，老人連一英寸都拉不上來。他的釣線很結實，是為釣大魚而做的。他用背抵住釣線，直至釣線繃得很緊，豆大的水珠從釣線上彈落下來。隨後釣線開始在水裡慢慢地發出嗞嗞聲。他依然緊握釣線，身子抵住橫坐板往後仰，頂住魚的拉力。小船開始慢慢地朝西北方向漂去。

這條魚不停地游著，魚和船在平靜的水面上慢慢前行。其他魚餌仍在水裡，不過沒有動靜，不需要操心。

"Now!" he said aloud and struck hard with both hands, gained a yard of line and then struck again and again, swinging with each arm alternately on the cord with all the strength of his arms and the pivoted weight of his body.

Nothing happened. The fish just moved away slowly and the old man could not raise him an inch. His line was strong and made for heavy fish and he held it against his back until it was so taut that beads of water were jumping from it. Then it began to make a slow hissing sound in the water and he still held it, bracing himself against the thwart and leaning back against the pull. The boat began to move slowly off toward the North-West.

The fish moved steadily and they travelled slowly on the calm water. The other baits were still in the water but there was nothing to be done.

「真希望那孩子在我身邊，」老人大聲說，「我被一條魚拖著，成了繫纜繩的樁子。我可以把釣線固定住，但那麼一來，魚就會繃斷釣線。我得拚命拉住，魚需要的時候就放一下。謝天謝地，魚在朝前游，沒有往底下鑽。」

要是往底下鑽，我該怎麼辦？我不知道。要是沉到水底，死在那裡怎麼辦？我不知道。不過，我得想些法子，有好多事情是我能做的。

他用背抵住釣線，看著它斜插進水裡。小船不停地往西北方向移動。

這會把它弄死的，老人想。它不可能永遠這麼游下去。可是四個小時之後，那條魚依然拖著小船不停地朝遠海游去。老人依然繃緊了斜背在肩上的釣線。

「我鉤住它的時候是中午，」他說，「可是我還從沒見過它呢。」

"I wish I had the boy," the old man said aloud. "I'm being towed by a fish and I'm the towing bitt. I could make the line fast. But then he could break it. I must hold him all I can and give him line when he must have it. Thank God he is travelling and not going down."

What I will do if he decides to go down, I don't know. What I'll do if he sounds and dies I don't know. But I'll do something. There are plenty of things I can do.

He held the line against his back and watched its slant in the water and the skiff moving steadily to the North-West.

This will kill him, the old man thought. He can't do this forever. But four hours later the fish was still swimming steadily out to sea, towing the skiff, and the old man was still braced solidly with the line across his back.

"It was noon when I hooked him," he said. "And I have never seen him."

他鉤住魚之前，就已經把草帽拉得低低地緊扣在頭上，這時草帽擦得額頭生疼。他還覺得口渴，於是便雙膝跪地，小心不去猛拉釣線，身子盡量往船頭移動，一隻手拿起了水瓶。他打開瓶子，喝了點水。接著便靠在船頭歇息，坐在取下的桅杆和船帆上，竭力不去想什麼，只是堅持著。

然後他回頭瞧了瞧，卻看不見陸地。能不能看見都一樣，他想。我總能借著哈瓦那的燈光回家。離太陽下沉還有兩個小時，也許在這之前它就會上來。要是這會兒不上來，也許月亮升起時會上來。要不，也許太陽升起時會上來。我沒有抽筋，身子骨還很結實，而它卻嘴裡帶著鉤子。不過那是多大的魚呀，拉力會這麼大。它的嘴巴一定是緊緊被金屬絲鉤住了。真希望能看到它。就是看上一眼也好，好讓我知道是跟什麼樣的東西在搏鬥。

He had pushed his straw hat hard down on his head before he hooked the fish and it was cutting his forehead. He was thirsty too and he got down on his knees and, being careful not to jerk on the line, moved as far into the bow as he could get and reached the water bottle with one hand. He opened it and drank a little. Then he rested against the bow. He rested sitting on the unstepped mast and sail and tried not to think but only to endure.

Then he looked behind him and saw that no land was visible. That makes no difference, he thought. I can always come in on the glow from Havana. There are two more hours before the sun sets and maybe he will come up before that. If he doesn't maybe he will come up with the moon. If he does not do that maybe he will come up with the sunrise. I have no cramps and I feel strong. It is he that has the hook in his mouth. But what a fish to pull like that. He must have his mouth shut tight on the wire. I wish I could see him. I wish I could see him only once to know what I have against me.

老人憑觀察星星判斷，整個晚上那條魚既沒有改變路線，也沒有改變方向。日落後天氣很冷，老人背上、胳膊上和老腿上的汗水都已經乾了，身子發冷。白天，他已經把蓋著魚餌箱的麻袋拿起來，攤在太陽下曬乾了。太陽下去後，他用麻袋裹住脖子，袋子拖下來蓋在背上。他小心地將麻袋塞到斜背在肩上的釣線底下，讓麻袋墊著釣線，他變換了姿態，俯身靠在船頭上，幾乎是很舒服了。這個姿勢其實只是不那麼難受而已，他卻認為算是舒服了。

我奈何不了它，它也奈何不了我，他想。只要它這麼一直游下去，誰也奈何不了誰。

The fish never changed his course nor his direction all that night as far as the man could tell from watching the stars. It was cold after the sun went down and the old man's sweat dried cold on his back and his arms and his old legs. During the day he had taken the sack that covered the bait box and spread it in the sun to dry. After the sun went down he tied it around his neck so that it hung down over his back and he cautiously worked it down under the line that was across his shoulders now. The sack cushioned the line and he had found a way of leaning forward against the bow so that he was almost comfortable. The position actually was only somewhat less intolerable; but he thought of it as almost comfortable.

I can do nothing with him and he can do nothing with me, he thought. Not as long as he keeps this up.

有一次他站起來，隔著船沿小便，看了看星星，又查看了一下航路。釣線從他肩上筆直地垂下來，在水裡顯出一道磷光。現在魚和船移動得更慢了，哈瓦那的燈光已不再那麼明亮，所以他知道水流準將他們往東帶去。要是望不到哈瓦那的燈光，我們一定是往東走得更遠了，他想。如果魚的路線不變的話，準還要好幾個小時後才能看到燈光。不知道今天棒球大聯賽的結果怎樣，他想。幹我們這一行的，要有一台收音機該多美。隨後他想，老是想著這東西，想想你在幹的事，你絕不能幹蠢事。

接著他大聲說：「真希望那孩子在我身邊，幫幫我也見見這種場面。」

一旦上了年紀，誰都不該單槍匹馬了，他想。可是這又免不了。若要身強力壯，就得記著趁鮪魚還沒有壞就把它吃掉。記住，儘管你根本不想吃，你還是得在早晨吃下去。記住，他自言自語地說。

Once he stood up and urinated over the side of the skiff and looked at the stars and checked his course. The line showed like a phosphorescent streak in the water straight out from his shoulders. They were moving more slowly now and the glow of Havana was not so strong, so that he knew the current must be carrying them to the eastward. If I lose the glare of Havana we must be going more to the eastward, he thought. For if the fish's course held true I must see it for many more hours. I wonder how the baseball came out in the grand leagues today, he thought. It would be wonderful to do this with a radio. Then he thought, think of it always. Think of what you are doing. You must do nothing stupid.

Then he said aloud, "I wish I had the boy. To help me and to see this."

No one should be alone in their old age, he thought. But it is unavoidable. I must remember to eat the tuna before he spoils in order to keep strong. Remember, no matter how little you want to, that you must eat him in the morning. Remember, he said to himself.

夜裡兩條海豚來到小船附近，他聽得見它們翻滾和噴水的聲音，他能分辨得出雄海豚噴水的聲音和雌海豚歎息似的噴水聲。

「它們很不錯，」他說，「玩呀，鬧呀，相親相愛。它們像飛魚一樣，是我們的兄弟。」

隨後，他開始憐憫起上鉤的大魚來。它很了不起，也很奇特，誰知道它幾歲了，他想。我從來沒有釣到過力氣這麼大，行動這麼奇怪的魚。它也許是太聰明了，所以才沒有往上跳。要是跳起來或者瘋狂逃竄，那我可能就毀了。但是，也許它以前多次上過鉤，知道就該這麼對抗。它不可能知道同它鬥的就只有一個人，而且還是個老人。可是，這是一條多大的魚呀！要是魚肉好，在市場上能賺多少錢呀。它咬起餌來像條雄魚，拖起來也像是雄魚，對抗起來不慌不忙。不知道這是計謀呢，還是像我一樣已經絕望了呢？

During the night two porpoises came around the boat and he could hear them rolling and blowing. He could tell the difference between the blowing noise the male made and the sighing blow of the female.

"They are good," he said. "They play and make jokes and love one another. They are our brothers like the flying fish."

Then he began to pity the great fish that he had hooked. He is wonderful and strange and who knows how old he is, he thought. Never have I had such a strong fish nor one who acted so strangely. Perhaps he is too wise to jump. He could ruin me by jumping or by a wild rush. But perhaps he has been hooked many times before and he knows that this is how he should make his fight. He cannot know that it is only one man against him, nor that it is an old man. But what a great fish he is and what will he bring in the market if the flesh is good. He took the bait like a male and he pulls like a male and his fight has no panic in it. I wonder if he has any plans or if he is just as desperate as I am?

他還記得一對大旗魚中的一條上鉤的那一回。雄魚總是讓雌魚先吃餌，上鉤的那條雌魚拚命掙扎，既驚慌又絕望，很快便筋疲力盡了。而雄魚一直都陪伴著它，越過釣線，和它一起在水面打轉。雄魚靠得那麼近，老人擔心它的尾巴會將釣線割斷，那尾巴像鐮刀般鋒利，大小和模樣也都像鐮刀。老人用手鉤把雌魚鉤上來，抓住邊緣像砂紙一樣長劍般的嘴，對著頭頂敲打它，直到魚的顏色轉成鏡子襯裡的紅色。隨後又在男孩的幫助下把它拉到船上。而雄魚一直陪伴在船邊。後來老人在清理釣線、準備魚叉的時候，雄魚躍到了船邊上空，想看看雌魚在什麼地方。然後它鑽進深水，張開紫色的翅膀，也就是胸鰭，露出所有寬闊的紫色條紋。它很美，老人記得，而且它一直陪伴著雌魚。

這是我見過最傷心的一幕了，老人想。男孩也很傷心，我們請求雌魚的原諒後，迅速將它宰殺了。

He remembered the time he had hooked one of a pair of marlin. The male fish always let the female fish feed first and the hooked fish, the female, made a wild, panic-stricken, despairing fight that soon exhausted her, and all the time the male had stayed with her, crossing the line and circling with her on the surface. He had stayed so close that the old man was afraid he would cut the line with his tail which was sharp as a scythe and almost of that size and shape. When the old man had gaffed her and clubbed her, holding the rapier bill with its sandpaper edge and clubbing her across the top of her head until her colour turned to a colour almost like the backing of mirrors, and then, with the boy's aid, hoisted her aboard, the male fish had stayed by the side of the boat. Then, while the old man was clearing the lines and preparing the harpoon, the male fish jumped high into the air beside the boat to see where the female was and then went down deep, his lavender wings, that were his pectoral fins, spread wide and all his wide lavender stripes showing. He was beautiful, the old man remembered, and he had stayed.

That was the saddest thing I ever saw with them, the old man thought. The boy was sad too and we begged her pardon and butchered her promptly.

「要是那孩子在就好了。」他大聲說，靠在船頭的圓形木殼板上，透過斜背在肩上的釣線，他感覺到了大魚的力量。那條魚一直隨心所欲地游著。

我耍的花招逼它做出了選擇，老人想。

它選擇待在黑暗的深水裡，這樣一切圈套、陷阱和花招都奈何它不得。我選擇到誰都沒去過的地方找它，那個地方世界上誰也沒去過。此刻我們給拴在一起了，打從中午起就是這樣。我們雙方都沒有幫手。

也許我不該當漁夫，他想。不過，我是為這而生的。我必須要記著天亮後把鮪魚吃掉。

"I wish the boy was here," he said aloud and settled himself against the rounded planks of the bow and felt the strength of the great fish through the line he held across his shoulders moving steadily toward whatever he had chosen.

When once, through my treachery, it had been necessary to him to make a choice, the old man thought.

His choice had been to stay in the deep dark water far out beyond all snares and traps and treacheries. My choice was to go there to find him beyond all people. Beyond all people in the world. Now we are joined together and have been since noon. And no one to help either one of us.

Perhaps I should not have been a fisherman, he thought. But that was the thing that I was born for. I must surely remember to eat the tuna after it gets light.

天亮前某個時候，什麼東西咬了一下他身後的釣餌。他聽見竿子折斷了，釣線開始越過船舷往外飛馳。黑暗中，他解下帶鞘的刀，讓魚的拉力壓在左肩，身子往後仰，在船舷的木頭上割斷了釣線。隨後，他又割斷了最靠近他的另一根釣線，摸黑把兩根備用釣線的斷頭接好。他單手熟練地操作著，把線結抽緊時，他的一隻腳踩在釣線卷上，將它固定住。這樣，他就有六卷備用線了，兩卷是割斷兩個釣餌後得來的，還有兩卷連著大魚咬鉤的釣線，這些線都被接在一起了。

Some time before daylight something took one of the baits that were behind him. He heard the stick break and the line begin to rush out over the gunwale of the skiff. In the darkness he loosened his sheath knife and taking all the strain of the fish on his left shoulder he leaned back and cut the line against the wood of the gunwale. Then he cut the other line closest to him and in the dark made the loose ends of the reserve coils fast. He worked skillfully with the one hand and put his foot on the coils to hold them as he drew his knots tight. Now he had six reserve coils of line. There were two from each bait he had severed and the two from the bait the fish had taken and they were all connected.

天亮以後，他想，我要回頭再處理一下那條四十英尋深的帶釣餌的線，把它也切斷，接上備用線。我將損失二百英尋長的加泰羅尼亞優質釣線[9]，還有魚鉤和接鉤繩。這些倒是可以添置的。可要是我鉤住了其他魚，而讓這條魚跑了，那還有什麼辦法補救呢？我不知道現在上鉤的是條什麼魚。可能是條旗魚，或者是劍魚，要不就是鯊魚。我摸不透，我得盡快把它處理掉。

他大聲說：「真希望那孩子在這兒。」

可是那孩子不在，他想。就只有你自己，現在你還是回頭把最後一根釣線弄好吧，不管天黑不黑，把它割斷，然後接上兩卷備用線。

9 原文為西班牙語。

After it is light, he thought, I will work back to the forty-fathom bait and cut it away too and link up the reserve coils. I will have lost two hundred fathoms of good Catalan *cordel* and the hooks and leaders. That can be replaced. But who replaces this fish if I hook some fish and it cuts him off? I don't know what that fish was that took the bait just now. It could have been a marlin or a broadbill or a shark. I never felt him. I had to get rid of him too fast.

Aloud he said, "I wish I had the boy."

But you haven't got the boy, he thought. You have only yourself and you had better work back to the last line now, in the dark or not in the dark, and cut it away and hook up the two reserve coils.

他說幹就幹，但在黑暗中不好操作。一次，那條魚激起大浪，把他拖翻在地，臉朝下，眼睛下被割開了一條口子。鮮血從臉頰上流下，但卻凝結起來，還沒到下巴就乾了。他奮力回到船頭，靠著木板休息。他整了整麻袋，小心挪動了一下釣線，換了個部位將它斜背在肩上，用肩膀固定住。他小心地試探了一下魚的拉力，隨後又用手感覺了一下小船在水中行進的速度。

我不明白它幹麼要晃動，他想。金屬接鉤繩一定是滑到了它高高隆起的背上。當然，它的背不可能像我的背那樣難受。但是不管魚有多大，它總不能將小船永遠這麼拖下去。現在，一切可能引起麻煩的事情都解決了。而且我有充足的備用釣線以及一個男子漢所求的一切。

「魚呀，」他輕輕地說出聲來，「我會誓死奉陪到底。」

So he did it. It was difficult in the dark and once the fish made a surge that pulled him down on his face and made a cut below his eye. The blood ran down his cheek a little way. But it coagulated and dried before it reached his chin and he worked his way back to the bow and rested against the wood. He adjusted the sack and carefully worked the line so that it came across a new part of his shoulders and, holding it anchored with his shoulders, he carefully felt the pull of the fish and then felt with his hand the progress of the skiff through the water.

I wonder what he made that lurch for, he thought. The wire must have slipped on the great hill of his back. Certainly his back cannot feel as badly as mine does. But he cannot pull this skiff forever, no matter how great he is. Now everything is cleared away that might make trouble and I have a big reserve of line; all that a man can ask.

"Fish," he said softly, aloud, "I'll stay with you until I am dead."

我猜想，它也會陪著我，老人思忖道。他等待著天明。拂曉前很冷，他緊貼著木板取暖。它能撐多久，我也能撐多久，他想。天邊露出第一道光線時，釣線往外伸展，進入水中。小船不停地移動著。太陽露出第一道邊時，陽光射在老人的右肩上。

「它一直在朝北游，」老人說。水流會把我們遠遠地朝東沖去，他想。但願它會隨水流轉向，那就表明它累了。

太陽升得更高了，老人明白，大魚並不累。只有一個跡象對他有利：釣線的傾斜度表明，魚在水裡游的深度已經比先前淺了。這並不一定意味著它就會跳上來。不過，它也許會跳上來。

「天主呀，讓它跳吧，」老人說，「我有足夠的釣線對付它。」

也許，我可以拉得緊一點，它感到難受就會跳了，他想。既然天已經亮了，那就讓它跳吧，它脊骨上的氣囊會充滿空氣，那就無法潛入深海裡去死了。

He'll stay with me too, I suppose, the old man thought and he waited for it to be light. It was cold now in the time before daylight and he pushed against the wood to be warm. I can do it as long as he can, he thought. And in the first light the line extended out and down into the water. The boat moved steadily and when the first edge of the sun rose it was on the old man's right shoulder.

"He's headed north," the old man said. The current will have set us far to the eastward, he thought. I wish he would turn with the current. That would show that he was tiring.

When the sun had risen further the old man realized that the fish was not tiring. There was only one favorable sign. The slant of the line showed he was swimming at a lesser depth. That did not necessarily mean that he would jump. But he might.

"God let him jump," the old man said. "I have enough line to handle him."

Maybe if I can increase the tension just a little it will hurt him and he will jump, he thought. Now that it is daylight let him jump so that he'll fill the sacks along his backbone with air and then he cannot go deep to die.

他試著增加了拉力，但是自從魚上鉤以後，釣線已經繃得快要斷了。他身子往後仰去拉的時候，感覺到線已經繃得很緊，他心裡明白，不能再用勁了。我不能猛拉，他想。每猛拉一次，魚鉤割開的口子就會加大，那麼大魚一跳就可能會脫鉤。不管怎樣，太陽出來後我感覺好多了，終於不必眼朝太陽了。

釣線上掛著黃色的水草，但老人明白這只會增加魚的阻力，他心裡高興起來，這是黃色的馬尾藻，夜裡發出強烈的磷光。

「魚呀，」他說，「我喜歡你，也很尊敬你，但今天天黑之前，我要殺死你。」

希望如此，他想。

一隻小鳥從北面朝小船飛來。這是一隻刺嘴鶯，在水面上低低地飛著。老人看得出來，這隻鳥已經很疲倦了。

He tried to increase the tension, but the line had been taut up to the very edge of the breaking point since he had hooked the fish and he felt the harshness as he leaned back to pull and knew he could put no more strain on it. I must not jerk it ever, he thought. Each jerk widens the cut the hook makes and then when he does jump he might throw it. Anyway I feel better with the sun and for once I do not have to look into it.

There was yellow weed on the line but the old man knew that only made an added drag and he was pleased. It was the yellow Gulf weed that had made so much phosphorescence in the night.

"Fish," he said, "I love you and respect you very much. But I will kill you dead before this day ends."

Let us hope so, he thought.

A small bird came toward the skiff from the north. He was a warbler and flying very low over the water. The old man could see that he was very tired.

小鳥飛到船尾，在那兒歇息。接著它在老人的頭頂上轉圈，然後停在了釣線上，那兒更舒服些。

「你多大了？」老人問鳥兒，「是第一次上路？」

他說話的時候，鳥兒看著他。小鳥太疲倦了，甚至無心細瞧釣線，只顧搖搖晃晃在上面走著，纖細的腳爪緊緊攫住釣線。

「釣線很牢靠，」老人告訴它，「太牢靠了。一夜都沒有風，你不該那麼累。鳥兒們都怎麼啦？」

那是因為鷹，他想，鷹飛到海上來找鳥兒。但他沒有把這個告訴那隻鳥，反正它也聽不懂，但它很快就會領教鷹的厲害。

「好好休息吧，小鳥，」他說，「然後再出海，像所有男人，或者鳥兒，或者魚兒那樣，試試你的運氣。」

The bird made the stern of the boat and rested there. Then he flew around the old man's head and rested on the line where he was more comfortable.

"How old are you?" the old man asked the bird. "Is this your first trip?"

The bird looked at him when he spoke. He was too tired even to examine the line and he teetered on it as his delicate feet gripped it fast.

"It's steady," the old man told him. "It's too steady. You shouldn't be that tired after a windless night. What are birds coming to?"

The hawks, he thought, that come out to sea to meet them. But he said nothing of this to the bird who could not understand him anyway and who would learn about the hawks soon enough.

"Take a good rest, small bird," he said. "Then go in and take your chance like any man or bird or fish."

他的脊背僵硬了一夜，現在痛得很，說話使他振奮起來。

「要是你高興，就留在我家吧，小鳥，」他說，「很抱歉，我不能撐起帆，藉著微風送你回去。不過我現在有朋友陪伴了。」

就在這時，大魚猛地一拉，把老人拖得直往船頭倒去，要不是他早有防備，放出了一段釣線，很可能就被拖下海了。

釣線突然晃動時，小鳥飛了起來，老人都沒有看到它飛走。他用右手小心地摸了摸釣線，發現手在流血。

「什麼東西傷著魚了。」他大聲說。他把線往回拉，看看能否讓魚轉向。當他將線拉得快要繃斷的那一刻，他卻穩穩地把線握住了。他把身子往後仰，靠在拉緊的釣線上。

「現在你感覺到了吧，魚呀，」他說，「天知道，我也一樣。」

It encouraged him to talk because his back had stiffened in the night and it hurt truly now.

"Stay at my house if you like, bird," he said. "I am sorry I cannot hoist the sail and take you in with the small breeze that is rising. But I am with a friend."

Just then the fish gave a sudden lurch that pulled the old man down onto the bow and would have pulled him overboard if he had not braced himself and given some line.

The bird had flown up when the line jerked and the old man had not even seen him go. He felt the line carefully with his right hand and noticed his hand was bleeding.

"Something hurt him then," he said aloud and pulled back on the line to see if he could turn the fish. But when he was touching the breaking point he held steady and settled back against the strain of the line.

"You're feeling it now, fish," he said. "And so, God knows, am I."

這時他舉目四顧，尋找那隻小鳥，因為他想有個伴兒。小鳥已經飛走了。

你沒有待多久，老人想。除非你上了岸，不然你去的地方會更加艱難。魚只猛拉了一下，我怎麼就讓魚割傷了呢？我準是愈來愈蠢了。或者也許是我只顧著看那隻小鳥，光惦記著它了。現在我要專心幹活了，然後我還得把鮪魚吃掉，免得力不從心。

「要是那孩子在這兒，還有一點鹽就好了。」他大聲說。

他把釣線的重量轉移到左肩，小心地跪下來，在海裡洗起手來，他把手浸在水裡有一分多鐘，看著鮮血漂散，看著小船移動時海水不停地拍打著他的手。

「這魚慢多了。」他說。

He looked around for the bird now because he would have liked him for company. The bird was gone.

You did not stay long, the man thought. But it is rougher where you are going until you make the shore. How did I let the fish cut me with that one quick pull he made? I must be getting very stupid. Or perhaps I was looking at the small bird and thinking of him. Now I will pay attention to my work and then I must eat the tuna so that I will not have a failure of strength.

"I wish the boy were here and that I had some salt," he said aloud.

Shifting the weight of the line to his left shoulder and kneeling carefully he washed his hand in the ocean and held it there, submerged, for more than a minute watching the blood trail away and the steady movement of the water against his hand as the boat moved.

"He has slowed much," he said.

老人本想把手在鹽水裡浸得更久些，但他擔心大魚又會猛拉釣線，於是站了起來，振作精神，舉起手遮住陽光。不過是讓釣線勒了一下，割破了肉。但那是用勁的地方。他知道在這事兒了結之前，還用得著這雙手。他不想還沒開始就負傷。

「現在，」手曬乾了後，他說，「我得把小鮪魚吃掉，利用手鉤，我能搆得著鮪魚，可以在這兒舒舒服服地吃。」

他跪了下來，用手鉤鉤住了船尾的鮪魚，朝自己拖過來，始終避開成卷的釣線。他再次用左肩扛住釣線，頂在左手和左胳膊上，然後從手鉤的鉤子上脫下鮪魚，把手鉤放回原地。他用一個膝蓋壓住魚身，沿著魚脖子到尾巴縱向剖魚，切出一條條暗紅色的肉來。這些魚條呈楔形，他從緊靠脊骨的地方一直切到魚肚子邊上。他割下六條，攤在船頭的木板上，在褲子上抹了抹小刀，逮住魚尾巴，提起魚骨，扔到了海裡。

The old man would have liked to keep his hand in the salt water longer but he was afraid of another sudden lurch by the fish and he stood up and braced himself and held his hand up against the sun. It was only a line burn that had cut his flesh. But it was in the working part of his hand. He knew he would need his hands before this was over and he did not like to be cut before it started.

"Now," he said, when his hand had dried, "I must eat the small tuna. I can reach him with the gaff and eat him here in comfort."

He knelt down and found the tuna under the stern with the gaff and drew it toward him keeping it clear of the coiled lines. Holding the line with his left shoulder again, and bracing on his left hand and arm, he took the tuna off the gaff hook and put the gaff back in place. He put one knee on the fish and cut strips of dark red meat longitudinally from the back of the head to the tail. They were wedge-shaped strips and he cut them from next to the back bone down to the edge of the belly. When he had cut six strips he spread them out on the wood of the bow, wiped his knife on his trousers, and lifted the carcass of the bonito by the tail and dropped it overboard.

「我想一整條是吃不了的。」說著他在一根魚條上橫著劃了一刀。他能感覺到釣線一陣陣拉動得厲害，而他的左手抽筋了。這隻手緊拉著沉重的釣線，他厭惡地瞧了瞧自己的左手。

「這算什麼手呀，」他說，「你樂意抽筋就抽吧。把自己弄得像爪子一樣，對你沒有什麼好處。」

來吧，他想，他朝黑暗的海水裡望去，看著傾斜的釣線。現在把它吃下去吧，這會讓你的手有力氣的。你的手並沒有過錯，而且你已經和魚對峙好多個小時了。但你是能奉陪到底的。現在就把鮪魚吃掉吧。

他撿起一片魚，放進嘴裡，慢慢地咀嚼著，並不覺得難吃。

好好嚼吧，他想，把汁水都吃掉。要是能加點酸橙，或者檸檬，或者鹽倒是不壞。

"I don't think I can eat an entire one," he said and drew his knife across one of the strips. He could feel the steady hard pull of the line and his left hand was cramped. It drew up tight on the heavy cord and he looked at it in disgust.

"What kind of a hand is that," he said. "Cramp then if you want. Make yourself into a claw. It will do you no good."

Come on, he thought and looked down into the dark water at the slant of the line. Eat it now and it will strengthen the hand. It is not the hand's fault and you have been many hours with the fish. But you can stay with him forever. Eat the bonito now.

He picked up a piece and put it in his mouth and chewed it slowly. It was not unpleasant.

Chew it well, he thought, and get all the juices. It would not be bad to eat with a little lime or with lemon or with salt.

「感覺怎麼樣，手？」他問抽筋的手，那隻手幾乎已硬得像僵硬的死屍，「我要為你再吃些魚下去。」

他把切成了兩半的那片魚的另外一半也吃了，先細細地嚼著，然後把魚皮吐了出來。

「效果怎麼樣，手？是不是還沒到時候，沒法知道？」

他又拿起了一整片，嚼了起來。

「這條魚很強壯，血色也好，」他想，「我很幸運弄到了它，而不是鬼頭刀，鬼頭刀太甜。這魚幾乎沒有甜味，力氣還全在裡面。」

除了實惠，別的都沒有什麼意思，他想。要是有點鹽就好了。我不知道太陽是會把剩下的魚曬爛掉，還是曬乾，所以還是吃光好，儘管我還不餓。那條大魚很平靜，也很安穩。我要把魚全吃掉，這樣，我就能對付那條大魚了。

"How do you feel, hand?" he asked the cramped hand that was almost as stiff as rigor mortis. "I'll eat some more for you."

He ate the other part of the piece that he had cut in two. He chewed it carefully and then spat out the skin.

"How does it go, hand? Or is it too early to know?"

He took another full piece and chewed it.

"It is a strong full-blooded fish," he thought. "I was lucky to get him instead of dolphin. Dolphin is too sweet. This is hardly sweet at all and all the strength is still in it."

There is no sense in being anything but practical though, he thought. I wish I had some salt. And I do not know whether the sun will rot or dry what is left, so I had better eat it all although I am not hungry. The fish is calm and steady. I will eat it all and then I will be ready.

「忍耐一下吧，手，」他說，「我這麼做是為了你。」

我真希望能餵這條大魚，他想。它是我的兄弟。但我得把它殺死，而且得精力充沛地幹這事兒。他慢慢地專心地吃掉了全部楔形魚條。

他直起腰來，在褲子上抹了抹手。

「現在，」他說，「你可以把釣線放掉了，手啊。我會單用右臂跟它幹，直到你停止胡鬧。」他用左腳踩住抓在左手裡的沉重釣線，身子往後靠，用背部來頂住釣線的拉力。

「天主保佑我，別再讓我抽筋了，」他說，「因為我不知道魚會幹什麼。」

但是它似乎很平靜，他想，而且在按計畫行動。可是，它有什麼計畫呢，他想。我又有什麼計畫呢？因為它的個兒大，我的計畫得隨它的計畫而改變。要是它往上跳，我可以殺死它。但是它卻始終待在下面，那我也只好奉陪到底。

"Be patient, hand," he said. "I do this for you."

I wish I could feed the fish, he thought. He is my brother. But I must kill him and keep strong to do it. Slowly and conscientiously he ate all of the wedge-shaped strips of fish.

He straightened up, wiping his hand on his trousers.

"Now," he said. "You can let the cord go, hand, and I will handle him with the right arm alone until you stop that nonsense." He put his left foot on the heavy line that the left hand had held and lay back against the pull against his back.

"God help me to have the cramp go," he said. "Because I do not know what the fish is going to do."

But he seems calm, he thought, and following his plan. But what is his plan, he thought. And what is mine? Mine I must improvise to his because of his great size. If he will jump I can kill him. But he stays down forever. Then I will stay down with him forever.

他在褲子上擦了擦抽筋的手，想疏鬆一下手指。可是他的手沒能張開。也許太陽升起的時候手會張開，他想。也許要等生猛的鮪魚消化後才能張開。要是我非得用這隻手，那我就會打開它，不惜一切代價。但是現在，我不想硬把它打開。讓它自動打開，心甘情願地恢復吧。畢竟在夜裡不得不解開幾根釣線時，我用手過度了。

他目光橫掃海面，明白此刻自己是多麼孤獨。可是，他已能看到黑色深海裡的折光了，看到釣線往前伸展，看見平靜的海面上波濤奇怪地起伏。此刻，貿易風颳得烏雲集結了起來。他往前看去，只見一群野鴨越過水面，在天空的映襯下露出清晰的身影，然後模糊了，然後又清晰起來。他明白，在海上誰也不會感到孤單。

他想起來，有些人就怕乘著小船離開陸地，他知道現在正處於天氣突然變壞的季節。而現在他們正碰上颶風季節，沒有颶風的時候，颶風季節的天氣是一年中最好的。

He rubbed the cramped hand against his trousers and tried to gentle the fingers. But it would not open. Maybe it will open with the sun, he thought. Maybe it will open when the strong raw tuna is digested. If I have to have it, I will open it, cost whatever it costs. But I do not want to open it now by force. Let it open by itself and come back of its own accord. After all I abused it much in the night when it was necessary to free and untie the various lines.

He looked across the sea and knew how alone he was now. But he could see the prisms in the deep dark water and the line stretching ahead and the strange undulation of the calm. The clouds were building up now for the trade wind and he looked ahead and saw a flight of wild ducks etching themselves against the sky over the water, then blurring, then etching again and he knew no man was ever alone on the sea.

He thought of how some men feared being out of sight of land in a small boat and knew they were right in the months of sudden bad weather. But now they were in hurricane months and, when there are no hurricanes, the weather of hurricane months is the best of all the year.

颶風來臨的前幾天，要是你在海上，就可以在天空中看到徵兆。在岸上，人們是看不到的，因為不知道該看什麼，他想。陸地上也會出現異常，雲彩的形狀就會不同。但現在是不會有颶風的。

他望了望天空，只見白色的積雲已經生成，像一堆誘人的霜淇淋。高高的上空，九月高遠的天際映襯著薄薄的羽毛般的卷雲。

「微風[10]來了，」他說，「魚呀，這樣的天氣對我比對你更有利。」

他的左手還在抽筋，但正在慢慢地鬆開。

我討厭抽筋，他想。這是跟自己的身體過不去。要是食物中毒，當著別人拉肚子或者嘔吐是很丟臉的。但是抽筋——他把它叫做 calambre[11]——是對自己的羞辱，尤其是孤身一人的時候。

---

10 原文為西班牙語。

11 西班牙語，意為「抽筋」。

If there is a hurricane you always see the signs of it in the sky for days ahead, if you are at sea. They do not see it ashore because they do not know what to look for, he thought. The land must make a difference too, in the shape of the clouds. But we have no hurricane coming now.

He looked at the sky and saw the white cumulus built like friendly piles of ice cream and high above were the thin feathers of the cirrus against the high September sky.

"Light *brisa*," he said. "Better weather for me than for you, fish."

His left hand was still cramped, but he was unknotting it slowly.

I hate a cramp, he thought. It is a treachery of one's own body. It is humiliating before others to have a diarrhoea from ptomaine poisoning or to vomit from it. But a cramp, he thought of it as a *calambre*, humiliates oneself especially when one is alone.

那孩子要是在這兒，就可以替我揉一揉了，從前臂往下，鬆一鬆手，他想。不過手終究還是會鬆開的。

那時他還沒看到水中釣線的傾斜度已經變了，右手就已經感覺到拉力的變化。隨後他靠在釣線上，左手快速有力地拍打著大腿的時候，看見釣線慢慢地往上傾斜。

「它上來了，」他說，「張開吧，手呀。請你張開。」

釣線慢慢地不斷往上升，接著，小船前方的洋面鼓了起來，大魚露頭了。它不停地冒出來，海水從身子兩側瀉下。太陽下，大魚亮晃晃的，頭部和背部為深紫色。在陽光的照射下，魚身兩側的條紋顯得很寬，帶著淡紫色。它劍狀的嘴像棒球棒那麼長，由粗變細，活像一把長劍。它從水裡鑽出來，露出整個身體，隨後又像潛水夫那樣流暢地再次滑入水中。老人看到大鐮刀般的尾巴鑽了下去，釣線開始飛速往外躥。

If the boy were here he could rub it for me and loosen it down from the forearm, he thought. But it will loosen up.

Then, with his right hand he felt the difference in the pull of the line before he saw the slant change in the water. Then, as he leaned against the line and slapped his left hand hard and fast against his thigh he saw the line slanting slowly upward.

"He's coming up," he said. "Come on hand. Please come on."

The line rose slowly and steadily and then the surface of the ocean bulged ahead of the boat and the fish came out. He came out unendingly and water poured from his sides. He was bright in the sun and his head and back were dark purple and in the sun the stripes on his sides showed wide and a light lavender. His sword was as long as a baseball bat and tapered like a rapier and he rose his full length from the water and then re-entered it, smoothly, like a diver and the old man saw the great scythe-blade of his tail go under and the line commenced to race out.

「它比我的小船長兩英尺。」老人說。釣線往外拉得很快，但又很穩，大魚還沒有驚慌。老人用雙手拉住釣線，發力正好，不會將釣線拉斷。他知道要是他不能穩步施壓，使大魚減速，這條魚很可能會拉光所有的釣線，並把它拉斷。

它是條大魚，我得使它信服，他想。我決不能讓它知道自己有多大力量，或者一旦逃起來有多大能耐。我要是它，此刻會使出渾身力氣跑掉，直到拉斷釣線。不過，謝天謝地，它們並不像要殺死它們的人那麼聰明，儘管它們更高尚，更有能力。

老人見過很多大魚。他見過很多超過一千磅的魚，此生還捉到過兩條那麼大的魚，但從來不是單槍匹馬的。而現在，他看不見陸地，又和他所見過最大的魚拴在一起，這條魚比他聽說過的任何一條都要大，而且他的左手依然緊縮得像抓緊的鷹爪。

"He is two feet longer than the skiff," the old man said. The line was going out fast but steadily and the fish was not panicked. The old man was trying with both hands to keep the line just inside of breaking strength. He knew that if he could not slow the fish with a steady pressure the fish could take out all the line and break it.

He is a great fish and I must convince him, he thought. I must never let him learn his strength nor what he could do if he made his run. If I were him I would put in everything now and go until something broke. But, thank God, they are not as intelligent as we who kill them; although they are more noble and more able.

The old man had seen many great fish. He had seen many that weighed more than a thousand pounds and he had caught two of that size in his life, but never alone. Now alone, and out of sight of land, he was fast to the biggest fish that he had ever seen and bigger than he had ever heard of, and his left hand was still as tight as the gripped claws of an eagle.

不過左手的抽筋會好的，他想。肯定會鬆開，來幫助右手的。有三件東西彼此是兄弟：魚和我的雙手。它得恢復，真沒用，竟會抽筋。這條魚又慢下來了，按它平常的速度繼續游。

我不明白它為什麼會跳，老人想。它跳起來，幾乎像是要讓我瞧瞧它有多大。無論如何，我現在明白了，他想。我真希望能讓它看看我是怎樣一個人。但那樣它會看到我的手在抽筋。讓它認為我比現在的我更有男子氣概吧，我會是那樣的。但願我是那條魚，他想，那樣就可以利用它的一切僅僅是對付我的意志和智慧。

他舒適地靠在木板上，忍受著發作時的疼痛。而這條魚穩穩地游著，小船慢慢劃過深色的海水。東風起了，海上泛起小小的波濤。中午時分，老人的左手不再抽筋了。

「魚呀，對你來說，這是個壞消息。」他說完把蓋著肩膀的麻袋上的釣線移了移。

It will uncramp though, he thought. Surely it will uncramp to help my right hand. There are three things that are brothers: the fish and my two hands. It must uncramp. It is unworthy of it to be cramped. The fish had slowed again and was going at his usual pace.

I wonder why he jumped, the old man thought. He jumped almost as though to show me how big he was. I know now, anyway, he thought. I wish I could show him what sort of man I am. But then he would see the cramped hand. Let him think I am more man than I am and I will be so. I wish I was the fish, he thought, with everything he has against only my will and my intelligence.

He settled comfortably against the wood and took his suffering as it came and the fish swam steadily and the boat moved slowly through the dark water. There was a small sea rising with the wind coming up from the east and at noon the old man's left hand was uncramped.

"Bad news for you, fish," he said and shifted the line over the sacks that covered his shoulders.

他很舒服，但也很痛苦，儘管他根本不承認痛苦。

「我不信教，」他說，「但我要說十遍《天主經》和十遍《聖母經》，好讓我抓住這條魚，而且我答應，如果我抓住了它，我一定到科伯聖母那兒去朝聖。我許願。」

他開始刻板地祈禱起來，有時累得忘了禱告詞便說得很快，好順口而出。《聖母經》比《天主經》容易說，他想。

「大恩大德的馬利亞，天主與你同在。你是女人中有福的。你生命的果實耶穌也是有福的。聖靈馬利亞，聖母馬利亞，替我們這些罪人，現在和臨終時刻祈禱吧。阿門。」接著，他又說：「萬福聖母馬利亞，為這條魚的死亡祈禱吧，儘管它很了不起。」

做完了禱告，他感覺好多了，但痛楚依然，也許還更糟一點。他倚在船頭的木板上，開始機械地活動起左手的手指來。

He was comfortable but suffering, although he did not admit the suffering at all.

"I am not religious," he said. "But I will say ten Our Fathers and ten Hail Marys that I should catch this fish, and I promise to make a pilgrimage to the Virgen de Cobre if I catch him. That is a promise."

He commenced to say his prayers mechanically. Sometimes he would be so tired that he could not remember the prayer and then he would say them fast so that they would come automatically. Hail Marys are easier to say than Our Fathers, he thought.

"Hail Mary full of Grace the Lord is with thee. Blessed art thou among women and blessed is the fruit of thy womb, Jesus. Holy Mary, Mother of God, pray for us sinners now and at the hour of our death. Amen." Then he added, "Blessed Virgen, pray for the death of this fish. Wonderful though he is."

With his prayers said, and feeling much better, but suffering exactly as much, and perhaps a little more, he leaned against the wood of the bow and began, mechanically, to work the fingers of his left hand.

這時微風徐來，太陽卻還是很熱。

「我還是再給船尾外頭的那條小釣線裝上釣餌吧，」他說，「要是這條魚決心再待上一夜，那我要再吃些東西，而且瓶裡的水也不多了。我想這兒只能搞到鬼頭刀。要是趁著新鮮的時候吃，鬼頭刀也不壞。真希望今晚會有一條飛魚落到船裡。可是我沒有光來引誘飛魚。飛魚生吃味道好極了，又不需要切成塊。現在我得保存所有力氣。天主呀，我不知道它會那麼大。」

「我還是要把它宰了，」他說，「不管它有多麼偉大和榮耀。」

不過這不公平，他想。但是我要讓它看看，一個男子漢有多大能耐，有多少耐力。

「我告訴過那孩子，我是個怪老頭，」他說，「現在是我必須證明這話的時候了。」

The sun was hot now although the breeze was rising gently.

"I had better re-bait that little line out over the stern," he said. "If the fish decides to stay another night I will need to eat again and the water is low in the bottle. I don't think I can get anything but a dolphin here. But if I eat him fresh enough he won't be bad. I wish a flying fish would come on board tonight. But I have no light to attract them. A flying fish is excellent to eat raw and I would not have to cut him up. I must save all my strength now. Christ, I did not know he was so big."

"I'll kill him though," he said. "In all his greatness and his glory."

Although it is unjust, he thought. But I will show him what a man can do and what a man endures.

"I told the boy I was a strange old man," he said. "Now is when I must prove it."

他已經證明了上千次，但這並不說明什麼。現在，他正在再次證明。每一次都是新的一次，而每次證明的時候他從不回想過去。

但願它會睡著，那樣我也可以睡了，可以夢見獅子，他想。為什麼獅子成了留下的主要念想呢？別想了，老傢伙，他自言自語。輕輕地靠在木板上休息，什麼也別想。它正在忙著呢。你可要盡量少動。

快到下午了，船還是又慢又穩地移動著。但現在，微微的東風給船增添了阻力，老人駕著細浪，輕悠悠地漂流。斜背在肩上的釣線引起的傷痛變得舒緩而平和。

下午有一回釣線開始上升。但那條魚只不過是在稍高一點的地方繼續游罷了。太陽照在老人的左臂、左肩和背部，他據此判斷，魚已經轉到東北方向了。

The thousand times that he had proved it meant nothing. Now he was proving it again. Each time was a new time and he never thought about the past when he was doing it.

I wish he'd sleep and I could sleep and dream about the lions, he thought. Why are the lions the main thing that is left? Don't think, old man, he said to himself. Rest gently now against the wood and think of nothing. He is working. Work as little as you can.

It was getting into the afternoon and the boat still moved slowly and steadily. But there was an added drag now from the easterly breeze and the old man rode gently with the small sea and the hurt of the cord across his back came to him easily and smoothly.

Once in the afternoon the line started to rise again. But the fish only continued to swim at a slightly higher level. The sun was on the old man's left arm and shoulder and on his back. So he knew the fish had turned east of north.

那條魚老人已經見過一次，所以能想像出它在水裡游的樣子，紫色的胸鰭像翅膀一樣張開，筆直的大尾巴劃破幽暗的海水。不知道它在那麼深的海裡能看見多少，老人想。它的視力很好，馬的視力雖然要差得多，卻也能看見黑暗裡的東西。以前我在黑暗中也能看得很清楚，不過不是那種一團漆黑的地方，那時候我的視力差不多跟貓一樣好。

由於陽光的作用以及手指不斷的活動，他的左手現在一點都不抽筋了。他開始把更多的負擔轉移到左手，他聳了聳肩上的肌肉，稍稍擺脫了一點釣線造成的傷痛。

「魚呀，要是你還不累，」他大聲說，「你一定是不同尋常的了。」

這時他已經很累。他知道夜會很快到來。他竭力要想些別的事情，他想起了大聯賽，用他的話說就是Gran Ligas[12]，他知道紐約洋基隊在和底特律老虎隊[13]比賽。

12 西班牙語，意為「大聯賽」。

Now that he had seen him once, he could picture the fish swimming in the water with his purple pectoral fins set wide as wings and the great erect tail slicing through the dark. I wonder how much he sees at that depth, the old man thought. His eye is huge and a horse, with much less eye, can see in the dark. Once I could see quite well in the dark. Not in the absolute dark. But almost as a cat sees.

The sun and his steady movement of his fingers had uncramped his left hand now completely and he began to shift more of the strain to it and he shrugged the muscles of his back to shift the hurt of the cord a little.

"If you're not tired, fish," he said aloud, "you must be very strange."

He felt very tired now and he knew the night would come soon and he tried to think of other things. He thought of the Big Leagues, to him they were the *Gran Ligas*, and he knew that the Yankees of New York were playing the *Tigres* of Detroit.

現在比賽已進入第二天了，我還不知道比賽[14]的結果，他想。但我得有信心，要對得起名將迪馬喬，他幹什麼都完美，甚至腳跟上長了骨刺，痛得厲害也是這樣。骨刺是什麼東西？他問自己。Un espuela de hueso[15]。我們不長骨刺。它會不會像鬥雞腳上的距鐵扎進腳跟那麼疼？我想我忍受不了那種痛苦，我也不像鬥雞，被啄瞎了一隻眼睛或者兩眼都瞎了還能繼續戰鬥。和那些厲害的鳥獸相比，人算不得什麼。我寧願做待在黑暗的海底的那傢伙。

「除非有鯊魚要來，」他大聲說，「要是鯊魚來了，願天主憐憫它和我。」

你認為名將迪馬喬守著一條魚，能像我守這條魚這麼久嗎？他想。可以肯定他會，而且會守得更久，因為他年輕力壯。更何況他父親是個漁夫。但是那骨刺會讓他疼得受不了嗎？

13 原文為西班牙語。
14 原文為西班牙語。
15 西班牙語，意為「骨刺」。

This is the second day now that I do not know the result of the *juegos*, he thought. But I must have confidence and I must be worthy of the great DiMaggio who does all things perfectly even with the pain of the bone spur in his heel. What is a bone spur? he asked himself. *Un espuela de hueso*. We do not have them. Can it be as painful as the spur of a fighting cock in one's heel? I do not think I could endure that or the loss of the eye and of both eyes and continue to fight as the fighting cocks do. Man is not much beside the great birds and beasts. Still I would rather be that beast down there in the darkness of the sea.

"Unless sharks come," he said aloud. "If sharks come, God pity him and me."

Do you believe the great DiMaggio would stay with a fish as long as I will stay with this one? he thought. I am sure he would and more since he is young and strong. Also his father was a fisherman. But would the bone spur hurt him too much?

「我不知道，」他大聲說，「我從來沒有長過骨刺。」

太陽下去了。為了給自己鼓氣，他憶起了卡薩布蘭卡一家小酒店的情景。那時他同一個大塊頭黑人比手勁，那人來自西恩富戈斯，是碼頭上最強壯的人。他們拗了一天一夜，手肘撐在桌面的粉筆線上，前臂伸直，兩人的手緊緊抓住。雙方都想把對方的手壓倒在桌上。很多人都下了賭注。汽油燈下，人們進進出出。他瞧了瞧那黑人的胳膊、手和臉。雙方較量了八個小時之後，便每四個小時更換一次裁判，好讓裁判有時間睡覺。血從他和黑人的手指甲上湧出，雙方都盯住對方的眼睛、手和前臂。下注的人走進走出，坐在靠牆的高高的椅子上，觀看比賽。牆壁是木頭做的，漆成了鮮豔的藍色，燈把兩人的影子投到了牆上。

黑人的影子很大，微風吹動燈具時，影子在牆上搖曳。

"I do not know," he said aloud. "I never had a bone spur."

As the sun set he remembered, to give himself more confidence, the time in the tavern at Casablanca when he had played the hand game with the great negro from Cienfuegos who was the strongest man on the docks. They had gone one day and one night with their elbows on a chalk line on the table and their forearms straight up and their hands gripped tight. Each one was trying to force the other's hand down onto the table. There was much betting and people went in and out of the room under the kerosene lights and he had looked at the arm and hand of the negro and at the negro's face. They changed the referees every four hours after the first eight so that the referees could sleep. Blood came out from under the fingernails of both his and the negro's hands and they looked each other in the eye and at their hands and forearms and the bettors went in and out of the room and sat on high chairs against the wall and watched. The walls were painted bright blue and were of wood and the lamps threw their shadows against them.

The negro's shadow was huge and it moved on the wall as the breeze moved the lamps.

整個晚上優勢在兩人之間變來變去，他們給黑人餵蘭姆酒，還給他點了菸。蘭姆酒一下肚，那黑人會拚命使勁。一次，他把老人，當時還不是老人，而是冠軍[16]聖地牙哥，把他的手扳下去將近有三英寸。但是老人又把手扳了回來，形成雙方勢均力敵的態勢。那一刻他有把握擊敗黑人，那是個好人，一個偉大的運動員。天亮時，打賭的人要求把比賽判為平局，但裁判直搖頭。這時老人用足氣力，把黑人的手壓得低下去，低下去，直至落到了木桌板上。比賽從星期天早上開始，到星期一早上才結束。很多參賭的人要求以平局了結算了，因為他們都得去碼頭卸下一袋袋的糖，或者去哈瓦那煤礦公司幹活。要不然，人人都是想讓比賽進行到底的。但不管怎麼說，他結束了比賽，而且是趕在大家得去幹活之前。

16 原文為西班牙語。

The odds would change back and forth all night and they fed the negro rum and lighted cigarettes for him. Then the negro, after the rum, would try for a tremendous effort and once he had the old man, who was not an old man then but was Santiago *El Campeón*, nearly three inches off balance. But the old man had raised his hand up to dead even again. He was sure then that he had the negro, who was a fine man and a great athlete, beaten. And at daylight when the bettors were asking that it be called a draw and the referee was shaking his head, he had unleashed his effort and forced the hand of the negro down and down until it rested on the wood. The match had started on a Sunday morning and ended on a Monday morning. Many of the bettors had asked for a draw because they had to go to work on the docks loading sacks of sugar or at the Havana Coal Company. Otherwise everyone would have wanted it to go to a finish. But he had finished it anyway and before anyone had to go to work.

打那以後好長一段時間，人人都叫他冠軍。到了春天，又進行了一次回訪賽。不過這次賭注下得不多，老人輕而易舉地贏了，因為在第一場比賽中，他摧毀了那個西恩富戈斯黑人的信心。從那以後，他又參加了幾次比賽，後來就沒有再參加了。他確信，只要他很想擊敗誰，就能擊敗誰。他也確信，比手勁對用來釣魚的右手不好。在幾次練習賽中，他試著用左手。可是左手一直叛逆，不聽使喚，所以他不信任左手。

現在太陽會把左手烤熱的，他想。除非夜裡冷得厲害，它不該再抽筋了。天知道夜裡會發生什麼。

一架飛機飛過他的頭頂往邁阿密去，他瞧著飛機的影子驚起了一群群飛魚。

「有那麼多飛魚，就應該有鬼頭刀。」他說著把身子往後仰，靠在釣線上，看看能不能把魚拉近些。但是不行。釣線一直硬梆梆的，上面抖動著水珠，馬上就要斷裂。小船慢慢地往前移動，他瞧著飛機，直至它消失。

For a long time after that everyone had called him The Champion and there had been a return match in the spring. But not much money was bet and he had won it quite easily since he had broken the confidence of the negro from Cienfuegos in the first match. After that he had a few matches and then no more. He decided that he could beat anyone if he wanted to badly enough and he decided that it was bad for his right hand for fishing. He had tried a few practice matches with his left hand. But his left hand had always been a traitor and would not do what he called on it to do and he did not trust it.

The sun will bake it out well now, he thought. It should not cramp on me again unless it gets too cold in the night. I wonder what this night will bring.

An airplane passed over head on its course to Miami and he watched its shadow scaring up the schools of flying fish.

"With so much flying fish there should be dolphin," he said, and leaned back on the line to see if it was possible to gain any on his fish. But he could not and it stayed at the hardness and water-drop shivering that preceded breaking. The boat moved ahead slowly and he watched the airplane until he could no longer see it.

　　在飛機上一定會覺得很新奇，他想。從那個高度往下瞧，不知道海會像什麼樣子？要是飛得不太高，一定能望見魚。我想在兩百英尋的高度上慢慢地飛，從上面往下看魚。在捕龜船上，我爬上過桅頂橫杆，即便在那個高度也能看得見很多東西。從那兒看下來，鬼頭刀顯得更綠，你能看清它們的條紋和紫色的斑點，還有整個游動的魚群。為什麼在黑色的水流中快速游動的魚，背部都是紫色的，通常還有紫色的條紋和斑點？當然鬼頭刀之所以在水裡看上去是綠色的，是因為它實際上是金黃色的。但是鬼頭刀餓得發慌要吃食的時候，身子兩側就會像旗魚一樣透出紫色條紋。難道是因為發怒，或者游得更快的緣故？

It must be very strange in an airplane, he thought. I wonder what the sea looks like from that height? They should be able to see the fish well if they do not fly too high. I would like to fly very slowly at two hundred fathoms high and see the fish from above. In the turtle boats I was in the cross-trees of the mast-head and even at that height I saw much. The dolphin look greener from there and you can see their stripes and their purple spots and you can see all of the school as they swim. Why is it that all the fast-moving fish of the dark current have purple backs and usually purple stripes or spots? The dolphin looks green of course because he is really golden. But when he comes to feed, truly hungry, purple stripes show on his sides as on a marlin. Can it be anger, or the greater speed he makes that brings them out?

天快黑的時候，他們經過一大片馬尾藻。馬尾藻在微波細浪的海面上漂動，就彷彿大洋跟黃色毯子下某種東西在做愛。這時有一隻鬼頭刀在他的細釣線上咬餌。他初次看到鬼頭刀是它跳到空中的時候，在最後一縷陽光中，很像是真的金子，它在空中狂野地搖尾屈身，驚慌中一次次跳出水面，彷彿在做雜技表演。老人挪到船尾，蹲下身子，用右手和胳膊抓住粗釣線，左手把鬼頭刀往回拉，每拉回一段釣線，左腳就赤腳踩上去。魚到了船尾，絕望地左右亂竄，老人仰靠在船尾，提起那條帶紫色斑點、金光閃閃的魚，把它拉進船尾。魚嘴顫動著在鉤子上急促地張合不停，扁長的魚身、魚尾和魚頭在船底亂撞，直到老人猛擊金閃閃的魚頭，那條魚才打了個顫，不動了。

Just before it was dark, as they passed a great island of Sargasso weed that heaved and swung in the light sea as though the ocean were making love with something under a yellow blanket, his small line was taken by a dolphin. He saw it first when it jumped in the air, true gold in the last of the sun and bending and flapping wildly in the air. It jumped again and again in the acrobatics of its fear and he worked his way back to the stern and crouching and holding the big line with his right hand and arm, he pulled the dolphin in with his left hand, stepping on the gained line each time with his bare left foot. When the fish was at the stern, plunging and cutting from side to side in desperation, the old man leaned over the stern and lifted the burnished gold fish with its purple spots over the stern. Its jaws were working convulsively in quick bites against the hook and it pounded the bottom of the skiff with its long flat body, its tail and its head until he clubbed it across the shining golden head until it shivered and was still.

老人從魚鉤上取下魚，又裝上一條沙丁魚做釣餌，把釣線扔到海裡。接著，他慢慢地將身子挪回船頭，洗了洗左手，在褲子上擦了擦。隨後，他把沉重的釣線從右手轉移到左手，又在海水裡洗了洗右手，他看著太陽沉入大海，看著傾斜的粗釣線。

「它一點都沒有改變。」他說。但是看著流動的海水打在手上，他發現水流明顯慢了下來。

「我把兩根槳捆在一起，橫放在船尾，好讓那條魚在夜裡能慢下來，」他說，「它能熬夜，我也可以。」

還是過會兒把鬼頭刀的腸子去掉好，那樣能把血保留在魚肉裡，他想。這事可以過一會兒再辦，同時我還可以把槳綁在一起，增加些阻力。現在我還是讓魚保持安靜，日落時別太驚擾它。太陽下沉時，所有的魚都會感到難受。

The old man unhooked the fish, rebaited the line with another sardine and tossed it over. Then he worked his way slowly back to the bow. He washed his left hand and wiped it on his trousers. Then he shifted the heavy line from his right hand to his left and washed his right hand in the sea while he watched the sun go into the ocean and the slant of the big cord.

"He hasn't changed at all," he said. But watching the movement of the water against his hand he noted that it was perceptibly slower.

"I'll lash the two oars together across the stern and that will slow him in the night," he said. "He's good for the night and so am I. "

It would be better to gut the dolphin a little later to save the blood in the meat, he thought. I can do that a little later and lash the oars to make a drag at the same time. I had better keep the fish quiet now and not disturb him too much at sunset. The setting of the sun is a difficult time for all fish.

他在空中晾乾了手，隨後抓住釣線，身子盡量放鬆，頂住木板，讓釣線把自己往前拉，使小船和他承受同等的，甚至更多的拉力。

我在學著幹這種事，他想。至少是這部分活兒。另外，他又想起來了，這條魚從上鉤以後還沒有吃過東西，而它個兒又那麼大，吃得也會很多。我吃了整條鮪魚，明天我還要吃鬼頭刀。他把鬼頭刀叫做「黃金」[17]。也許我在掏魚腸的時候就該吃掉一些。這種魚比鮪魚要難吃，可是話得說回來，幹什麼都不容易。

「你感覺怎麼樣，魚？」他大聲問，「我感覺很好，左手好多了，又有夠我吃一天一夜的東西。魚呀，你就拖著船走吧。」

17 原文為西班牙語。

He let his hand dry in the air then grasped the line with it and eased himself as much as he could and allowed himself to be pulled forward against the wood so that the boat took the strain as much, or more, than he did.

I'm learning how to do it, he thought. This part of it anyway. Then too, remember he hasn't eaten since he took the bait and he is huge and needs much food. I have eaten the whole bonito. Tomorrow I will eat the dolphin. He called it *dorado*. Perhaps I should eat some of it when I clean it. It will be harder to eat than the bonito. But, then, nothing is easy.

"How do you feel, fish?" he asked aloud. "I feel good and my left hand is better and I have food for a night and a day. Pull the boat, fish."

他的感覺並不是真的很好，因為勒在背上的釣線引起的疼痛幾乎已經超越了疼痛，變成了他不信任的麻木。不過我經歷過比這更糟的事情，他想。我的手只不過割破了一點點，另一隻手已經不再抽筋了，我的雙腿沒有毛病，而且在食物上我現在也比它更有優勢。

這時天黑了。九月裡，太陽一下沉，天很快就黑了。他靠在船頭磨損了的木板上，盡情地休息。第一批星星出來了。他不知道獵戶座左下方那顆最亮的星的名字，但是他看到了這顆星，而且知道這些星星很快都會出來，他又有那些遙遠的朋友了。

「那條魚也是我的朋友，」他大聲說，「我從來沒有見過或者聽過這樣的魚。但是我得把它宰了。幸虧我們不必去宰星星。」

設想有人每天得去宰月亮，他想。月亮會逃走。但是設想有人每天得去宰太陽呢？我們生來就很幸運，他想。

He did not truly feel good because the pain from the cord across his back had almost passed pain and gone into a dullness that he mistrusted. But I have had worse things than that, he thought. My hand is only cut a little and the cramp is gone from the other. My legs are all right. Also now I have gained on him in the question of sustenance.

It was dark now as it becomes dark quickly after the sun sets in September. He lay against the worn wood of the bow and rested all that he could. The first stars were out. He did not know the name of Rigel but he saw it and knew soon they would all be out and he would have all his distant friends.

"The fish is my friend too," he said aloud. "I have never seen or heard of such a fish. But I must kill him. I am glad we do not have to try to kill the stars."

Imagine if each day a man must try to kill the moon, he thought. The moon runs away. But imagine if a man each day should have to try to kill the sun? We were born lucky, he thought.

接著他為那條沒有東西吃的大魚感到難過，但是難過歸難過，他要宰它的決心卻未減。它能餵飽多少人呀，他想。但是他們配吃它嗎？不，當然不配。它的行為、它偉大的尊嚴讓誰都不配吃它。

我不明白這些事兒，他想。好在我們不必去宰太陽，或者月亮，或者星星。生活在海上，宰殺我們真正的朋友，已經夠受的了。

現在他想，我得考慮一下阻力問題。這有利有弊。要是那條魚使起勁來，而船槳造成的阻力又在，小船就沒有那麼輕巧了，然後我會放出很長的釣線，魚也會因此逃走。小船的輕巧延長了我們雙方的痛苦，但這正是我的安全所在，因為魚的速度驚人，只不過沒有施展出來罷了。不管會發生什麼，我都得掏出鬼頭刀的腸子，免得整條魚變壞，並且吃一些魚補補身體。

Then he was sorry for the great fish that had nothing to eat and his determination to kill him never relaxed in his sorrow for him. How many people will he feed, he thought. But are they worthy to eat him? No, of course not. There is no one worthy of eating him from the manner of his behaviour and his great dignity.

I do not understand these things, he thought. But it is good that we do not have to try to kill the sun or the moon or the stars. It is enough to live on the sea and kill our true brothers.

Now, he thought, I must think about the drag. It has its perils and its merits. I may lose so much line that I will lose him, if he makes his effort and the drag made by the oars is in place and the boat loses all her lightness. Her lightness prolongs both our suffering but it is my safety since he has great speed that he has never yet employed. No matter what passes I must gut the dolphin so he does not spoil and eat some of him to be strong.

現在我要休息一個多小時，感覺一下，確保那條魚確實還結實，而且很安穩，然後再回到船尾去幹那活兒，再做決定。同時我還可以看看它有什麼動靜，是否有什麼變化。兩把船槳是個好招，不過現在到了穩扎穩打的時候了。這條魚還是很有本事，我看到魚鉤鉤住了嘴角，而它卻緊閉嘴巴。魚鉤的傷害算不得什麼，飢餓的煎熬以及跟一個它一無所知的對象較量才是根本問題。歇一下吧，老頭兒，等下趟活兒來了再幹。

他自己估摸歇了有兩個小時。月亮要到很晚才出來，他沒法判斷時間。他的休息也只是相比較而言，其實他沒有真正休息。他的肩上依然背負著魚的拉力，不過他把左手靠在船頭的舷邊，把魚的抵抗力愈來愈多地轉嫁給小船本身。

要是把釣線固定住的話，那會多簡單呀，他想。但魚只要一掙扎，線就會斷掉。我必須用身體緩衝釣線的拉力，而且雙手隨時準備放出一段釣線。

Now I will rest an hour more and feel that he is solid and steady before I move back to the stern to do the work and make the decision. In the meantime I can see how he acts and if he shows any changes. The oars are a good trick; but it has reached the time to play for safety. He is much fish still and I saw that the hook was in the corner of his mouth and he has kept his mouth tight shut. The punishment of the hook is nothing. The punishment of hunger, and that he is against something that he does not comprehend, is everything. Rest now, old man, and let him work until your next duty comes.

He rested for what he believed to be two hours. The moon did not rise now until late and he had no way of judging the time. Nor was he really resting except comparatively. He was still bearing the pull of the fish across his shoulders but he placed his left hand on the gunwale of the bow and confided more and more of the resistance to the fish to the skiff itself.

How simple it would be if I could make the line fast, he thought. But with one small lurch he could break it. I must cushion the pull of the line with my body and at all times be ready to give line with both hands.

「可是你還沒有睡過覺，老頭兒，」他大聲說，「已經半天一夜了，現在又是另外一天了，你還沒有睡過覺。要是它還安穩，你就得想個招兒睡一會兒。你不睡覺，腦子就會不清楚。」

我頭腦很清醒，他想。太清醒了，像我的星星兄弟們那麼清醒。但我還是得睡覺。它們睡覺，月亮和太陽都睡覺，某些波瀾不驚，海面平靜的日子，甚至連海洋都睡覺。

但是記住要睡覺，他想。一定要讓你自己睡覺，想個簡單可靠的辦法來處理釣線。現在回去收拾鬼頭刀吧。要是你一定得睡覺的話，把船槳綁起來增加阻力就太危險啦。

我不睡覺也行，他自言自語，不過會很危險。

他開始手膝並用爬回船尾，小心不去猛拉釣線。它也許是半睡半醒，他想。但我不要它歇下來，它得一直這樣拉到死。

"But you have not slept yet, old man," he said aloud. "It is half a day and a night and now another day and you have not slept. You must devise a way so that you sleep a little if he is quiet and steady. If you do not sleep you might become unclear in the head."

I'm clear enough in the head, he thought. Too clear. I am as clear as the stars that are my brothers. Still I must sleep. They sleep and the moon and the sun sleep and even the ocean sleeps sometimes on certain days when there is no current and a flat calm.

But remember to sleep, he thought. Make yourself do it and devise some simple and sure way about the lines. Now go back and prepare the dolphin. It is too dangerous to rig the oars as a drag if you must sleep.

I could go without sleeping, he told himself. But it would be too dangerous.

He started to work his way back to the stern on his hands and knees, being careful not to jerk against the fish. He may be half asleep himself, he thought. But I do not want him to rest. He must pull until he dies.

他回到船尾，轉過身來，讓左手抓住斜背在肩上的釣線，右手將刀拉出刀鞘。這時，星星很亮，他能看清鬼頭刀。他把刀插進魚頭，把魚從船尾下方拖了出來。他一隻腳踏在魚上，很快將它破開，從肛門一直破到下顎尖。隨後他放下刀，用右手去掏腸子，把腸子掏乾淨，把魚鰓全拉掉。他覺得魚胃在手裡沉甸甸、滑溜溜的，便把它剖開。裡面有兩條飛魚，硬挺挺的，很新鮮。他把兩條魚並排擺著，把魚腸和魚鰓丟到船外。這些東西沉入海水，留下了一條磷光。鬼頭刀身子冰冷，星光下露出痲風病人皮膚般的灰白色。老人右腳踩在魚頭上，剝下一邊的魚皮，然後把魚翻了個身，剝掉另外一邊的魚皮，把兩邊的魚肉從頭到尾割了下來。

他讓魚骨挨著船舷滑下去，看看水裡有沒有打旋。但只看到慢慢下沉的磷光。他回過身來，把兩條飛魚裹在兩塊魚肉裡面，把刀插回刀鞘。他慢慢地將身子挪回船頭。在釣線的重壓下，他彎著背，右手拿著魚肉。

Back in the stern he turned so that his left hand held the strain of the line across his shoulders and drew his knife from its sheath with his right hand. The stars were bright now and he saw the dolphin clearly and he pushed the blade of his knife into his head and drew him out from under the stern. He put one of his feet on the fish and slit him quickly from the vent up to the tip of his lower jaw. Then he put his knife down and gutted him with his right hand, scooping him clean and pulling the gills clear. He felt the maw heavy and slippery in his hands and he slit it open. There were two flying fish inside. They were fresh and hard and he laid them side by side and dropped the guts and the gills over the stern. They sank leaving a trail of phosphorescence in the water. The dolphin was cold and a leprous gray-white now in the starlight and the old man skinned one side of him while he held his right foot on the fish's head. Then he turned him over and skinned the other side and cut each side off from the head down to the tail.

He slid the carcass overboard and looked to see if there was any swirl in the water. But there was only the light of its slow descent. He turned then and placed the two flying fish inside the two fillets of fish and putting his knife back in its sheath, he worked his way slowly back to the bow. His back was bent with the weight of the line across it and he carried the fish in his right hand.

回到船頭，他把兩塊魚肉和兩條飛魚並排放在木板上。接著他把斜壓在肩上的釣線換了個位置，又用左手抓住釣線，把手靠在船舷上。隨後他身子側向一邊，在水裡洗起了飛魚，留意著海水打在手上的速度。他的手剝了魚皮後閃著磷光，他觀察著水流擊打他的手。水流不那麼急了。他在小船的船殼外板上擦手的時候，磷光閃閃的微粒在海面上漂浮著，慢慢地漂向船尾。

「它愈來愈累了，要不就是正在歇息，」老人說，「現在讓我吃掉鬼頭刀，休息一下，睡一會兒。」

星空下，夜愈來愈冷。他吃掉了半片鬼頭刀肉和一條去頭去腸的飛魚。

「要是燒熟吃的話，鬼頭刀是多好的魚呀，」他說，「而生吃，它又多麼蹩腳！下回要是不帶鹽或者酸橙的話，我就不上船了。」

Back in the bow he laid the two fillets of fish out on the wood with the flying fish beside them. After that he settled the line across his shoulders in a new place and held it again with his left hand resting on the gunwale. Then he leaned over the side and washed the flying fish in the water, noting the speed of the water against his hand. His hand was phosphorescent from skinning the fish and he watched the flow of the water against it. The flow was less strong and as he rubbed the side of his hand against the planking of the skiff, particles of phosphorus floated off and drifted slowly astern.

"He is tiring or he is resting," the old man said. "Now let me get through the eating of this dolphin and get some rest and a little sleep."

Under the stars and with the night colder all the time he ate half of one of the dolphin fillets and one of the flying fish, gutted and with its head cut off.

"What an excellent fish dolphin is to eat cooked," he said. "And what a miserable fish raw. I will never go in a boat again without salt or limes."

我要是有腦子的話，我就會整天往船頭潑水，讓它曬乾，變成鹽，他想。話得說回來，我是在太陽快下去時才釣到鬼頭刀的。不過還是準備不足。但我還是把它全都嚼下去了，也沒有反胃。

東邊的天空布滿了陰雲，他熟悉的星星也一顆顆消失了。看來彷彿他正掉進一個雲團大峽谷。風也息了。

「三、四天後，壞天氣就要來了，」他說，「不過今天晚上和明天不會。現在準備一下，睡一會兒吧，老頭兒，趁魚平靜安穩的時候。」

他右手緊握釣線，然後讓大腿抵著右手，斜倚著把渾身的重量壓在船頭的木板上。接著他把肩上的釣線拉低了一點，用左手撐住它。

If I had brains I would have splashed water on the bow all day and drying, it would have made salt, he thought. But then I did not hook the dolphin until almost sunset. Still it was a lack of preparation. But I have chewed it all well and I am not nauseated.

The sky was clouding over to the east and one after another the stars he knew were gone. It looked now as though he were moving into a great canyon of clouds and the wind had dropped.

"There will be bad weather in three or four days," he said. "But not tonight and not tomorrow. Rig now to get some sleep, old man, while the fish is calm and steady."

He held the line tight in his right hand and then pushed his thigh against his right hand as he leaned all his weight against the wood of the bow. Then he passed the line a little lower on his shoulders and braced his left hand on it.

釣線只要這麼撐著，右手就能把它握住，他想。睡著時要是釣線鬆了，往外滑去，我的左手就會把我弄醒。這樣右手會很辛苦，但它吃慣了苦。就是睡上二十分鐘或者半個小時也好。他俯身向前，整個身子緊緊夾住釣線，所有的重量都落在右手上，然後他就睡著了。

他沒有夢見獅子，卻夢見了一大群海豚，綿延八到十英里。這正是交配季節，海豚會高高地躥到空中，再落回躍起時留在水中的水渦裡。

後來他夢見自己躺在村裡的床上，而且颳起了強勁的北風，他很冷，右手麻木了，因為頭枕在了手上，不是枕頭上。

後來他開始夢見長長的黃色海灘，看見獅群中的第一頭獅子傍晚時下到了海灘。接著，其餘的獅子也來了。他把下巴靠在船頭的木板上。船拋了錨停在那裡，晚風徐徐吹向海面。他等著看更多的獅子下來，心裡很愉快。

My right hand can hold it as long as it is braced, he thought. If it relaxes in sleep my left hand will wake me as the line goes out. It is hard on the right hand. But he is used to punishment. Even if I sleep twenty minutes or a half an hour it is good. He lay forward cramping himself against the line with all of his body, putting all his weight onto his right hand, and he was asleep.

He did not dream of the lions but instead of a vast school of porpoises that stretched for eight or ten miles and it was in the time of their mating and they would leap high into the air and return into the same hole they had made in the water when they leaped.

Then he dreamed that he was in the village on his bed and there was a norther and he was very cold and his right arm was asleep because his head had rested on it instead of a pillow.

After that he began to dream of the long yellow beach and he saw the first of the lions come down onto it in the early dark and then the other lions came and he rested his chin on the wood of the bows where the ship lay anchored with the evening off-shore breeze and he waited to see if there would be more lions and he was happy.

月亮升起來已經好久了，但他還在睡，大魚平穩地拖著，小船掉進了雲彩的隧道裡。

他的右拳猛地砸在臉上，把他弄醒了，釣線從右手滑出去。左手已經失去了知覺，不過他用右手全力制動，釣線卻飛了出去。最後他的左手找到了釣線，他把身子往後仰，抵住線，背部和左手被釣線勒得火辣辣地痛。左手承受著全部拉力，被勒得很深。他回頭看了看線圈，看見釣線正順暢地放出去。就在這時，那條魚跳了起來，掀起巨大的海浪，隨後重重地落了下來。儘管釣線飛快地往外溜，老人也已把釣線拉得快要斷掉，而且一次次拉到這個地步，那魚還是一次次跳起來，小船也駛得很快。他被拉倒了，緊緊靠著船頭，臉貼在切成條的鬼頭刀上，動彈不得。

我們等的就是這個，他想。那現在就讓我們來承受吧。

要讓它為釣線付出代價，他想。要讓它為釣線付出代價。

The moon had been up for a long time but he slept on and the fish pulled on steadily and the boat moved into the tunnel of clouds.

He woke with the jerk of his right fist coming up against his face and the line burning out through his right hand. He had no feeling of his left hand but he braked all he could with his right and the line rushed out. Finally his left hand found the line and he leaned back against the line and now it burned his back and his left hand, and his left hand was taking all the strain and cutting badly. He looked back at the coils of line and they were feeding smoothly. Just then the fish jumped making a great bursting of the ocean and then a heavy fall. Then he jumped again and again and the boat was going fast although line was still racing out and the old man was raising the strain to breaking point and raising it to breaking point again and again. He had been pulled down tight onto the bow and his face was in the cut slice of dolphin and he could not move.

This is what we waited for, he thought. So now let us take it.

Make him pay for the line, he thought. Make him pay for it.

他看不見魚躍，只聽見海水迸裂和魚落下時巨大的濺水聲。釣線飛速送出，嚴重割傷了他的手。不過他一直知道這會發生，所以竭力讓釣線勒在長繭的部位，不讓它滑到手掌上，或者傷著手指。

那孩子要是在這兒，就會弄濕線圈，他想。是的。要是那孩子在這兒。要是那孩子在這兒。

釣線溜呀，溜呀，不停地溜出去，但現在慢了下來，他正讓魚為拖出的每英寸付出代價。這時他從木板上，從被臉壓碎的魚條裡抬起頭來。隨後跪在地上，慢慢地站了起來。他一直在放出釣線，但愈來愈慢。他挪動著，回到能用腳觸摸到但卻看不到的線圈那兒。剩下的釣線還很多，現在這條魚得克服摩擦力，把新線拉進水裡。

He could not see the fish's jumps but only heard the breaking of the ocean and the heavy splash as he fell. The speed of the line was cutting his hands badly but he had always known this would happen and he tried to keep the cutting across the calloused parts and not let the line slip into the palm nor cut the fingers.

If the boy was here he would wet the coils of line, he thought. Yes. If the boy were here. If the boy were here.

The line went out and out and out but it was slowing now and he was making the fish earn each inch of it. Now he got his head up from the wood and out of the slice of fish that his cheek had crushed. Then he was on his knees and then he rose slowly to his feet. He was ceding line but more slowly all the time. He worked back to where he could feel with his foot the coils of line that he could not see. There was plenty of line still and now the fish had to pull the friction of all that new line through the water.

是的，他想。它已經跳了十幾次了，背囊裡充滿空氣，不可能潛入深水，死在我沒法把它弄上來的地方。它很快就會打旋，那我就得對付它了。不知道它為什麼突然驚跳起來。可能是飢餓使它不顧一切，或者是夜裡受到了什麼驚嚇？也許它突然感到害怕了。可是它那麼鎮靜，那麼強壯，似乎信心十足，無所畏懼。真是奇怪。

「你最好也信心十足，無所畏懼，老頭兒，」他說，「你又把它逮住了，但卻收不回釣線。不過很快它得打旋。」

老人用左手和肩膀把魚控制住，彎下身子，用右手舀了些水，把臉上的碎鬼頭刀肉洗掉。他擔心這東西會弄得他噁心、嘔吐，然後喪失體力。洗完臉後，他又在船邊的海水裡洗了右手，在鹽水裡浸了一會兒，瞧著太陽升起前第一線曙光的來臨。它幾乎在朝東移動，他想。這說明它累了，在隨波逐流。很快它得打旋。到那時硬仗就開始了。

Yes, he thought. And now he has jumped more than a dozen times and filled the sacks along his back with air and he cannot go down deep to die where I cannot bring him up. He will start circling soon and then I must work on him. I wonder what started him so suddenly? Could it have been hunger that made him desperate, or was he frightened by something in the night? Maybe he suddenly felt fear. But he was such a calm, strong fish and he seemed so fearless and so confident. It is strange.

"You better be fearless and confident yourself, old man," he said. "You're holding him again but you cannot get line. But soon he has to circle."

The old man held him with his left hand and his shoulders now and stooped down and scooped up water in his right hand to get the crushed dolphin flesh off of his face. He was afraid that it might nauseate him and he would vomit and lose his strength. When his face was cleaned he washed his right hand in the water over the side and then let it stay in the salt water while he watched the first light come before the sunrise. He's headed almost east, he thought. That means he is tired and going with the current. Soon he will have to circle. Then our true work begins.

他估摸著右手在海水裡浸得夠長了，便抽了回來，瞧了瞧。

「還可以，」他說，「男子漢不在乎這點痛。」

他小心地抓住釣線，不讓它嵌進剛勒傷的地方，他挪了挪身子的重心，騰出左手，把左手浸入小船另一邊的海水中。

「你這隻手雖然沒用，但幹得還不壞。」他對左手說，「不過有一陣子，你可沒有幫上忙。」

為什麼我不是生來就有兩隻好手呢？他想。也許這是我的不是，我沒有好好訓練那隻手。但是天知道它曾有過足夠的學習機會。不過夜裡它幹得倒還不壞，只抽了一次筋。要是再抽，就讓釣線把它勒斷算了。

After he judged that his right hand had been in the water long enough he took it out and looked at it.

"It is not bad," he said. "And pain does not matter to a man."

He took hold of the line carefully so that it did not fit into any of the fresh line cuts and shifted his weight so that he could put his left hand into the sea on the other side of the skiff.

"You did not do so badly for something worthless," he said to his left hand. "But there was a moment when I could not find you."

Why was I not born with two good hands? he thought. Perhaps it was my fault in not training that one properly. But God knows he has had enough chances to learn. He did not do so badly in the night, though, and he has only cramped once. If he cramps again let the line cut him off.

想到這裡，他知道自己的腦子不清醒了，想起了要再嚼一些鬼頭刀。但是我不能這樣，他對自己說。與其因為嘔吐而喪失體力，還不如這樣昏頭昏腦好些呢。我也知道，就算我吃了，胃裡也留不住，因為我的臉都貼上去過了。我會把它留到緊急情況下吃，只要它還沒壞掉。但現在要透過補營養來長力氣已經晚了。你真傻，他對自己說，把另外一條飛魚吃了不就行了。

飛魚就在那兒，去了腸子，隨時都可以吃。他用左手撿起魚，吃了起來。他細細地嚼著骨頭，連尾巴都吃了下去。

飛魚的營養幾乎比其他的魚都要好，他想。至少它能讓我長力氣，我需要的就是這個。現在能做的都已經做了，他想。讓它開始打旋吧，讓戰鬥開始吧。

When he thought that he knew that he was not being clear-headed and he thought he should chew some more of the dolphin. But I can't, he told himself. It is better to be light-headed than to lose your strength from nausea. And I know I cannot keep it if I eat it since my face was in it. I will keep it for an emergency until it goes bad. But it is too late to try for strength now through nourishment. You're stupid, he told himself. Eat the other flying fish.

It was there, cleaned and ready, and he picked it up with his left hand and ate it chewing the bones carefully and eating all of it down to the tail.

It has more nourishment than almost any fish, he thought. At least the kind of strength that I need. Now I have done what I can, he thought. Let him begin to circle and let the fight come.

這是他出海以來太陽第三次升起了。這時候，魚開始打旋。

從傾斜的釣線上，他看不出魚在打旋，現在似乎還為時尚早。他只覺得釣線的拉力隱約有點鬆了。他開始用右手輕輕地拉了拉釣線。像平常一樣，釣線繃緊了，不過就在快要斷裂的時候，釣線卻開始往回收。他的肩膀和腦袋從釣線下鑽了出來。他開始又輕又穩地把釣線往回收，揮動著雙手，使出渾身氣力，他的身體和雙腿都來幫忙。他的兩條老腿和肩膀也隨著揮舞的雙手轉動著。

「這是個很大的圈子，」他說，「不過它確實是在打轉了。」

隨後釣線再也收不進來了，他拉住釣線不動，看見陽光下釣線上迸出了水珠。接著釣線開始往外拉了，老人跪了下來，很不情願地讓魚回到深暗的海水裡。

The sun was rising for the third time since he had put to sea when the fish started to circle.

He could not see by the slant of the line that the fish was circling. It was too early for that. He just felt a faint slackening of the pressure of the line and he commenced to pull on it gently with his right hand. It tightened, as always, but just when he reached the point where it would break, line began to come in. He slipped his shoulders and head from under the line and began to pull in line steadily and gently. He used both of his hands in a swinging motion and tried to do the pulling as much as he could with his body and his legs. His old legs and shoulders pivoted with the swinging of the pulling.

"It is a very big circle," he said. "But he is circling."

Then the line would not come in any more and he held it until he saw the drops jumping from it in the sun. Then it started out and the old man knelt down and let it go grudgingly back into the dark water.

「現在它正旋轉到了圈子的最遠處。」他說。我得用足力氣拉住釣線，他想。每一次用勁拉都會縮小它轉的圈子。也許一個小時之後我就會看到它。現在我必須馴服它，然後宰了它。

但是這條魚繼續慢慢地轉著圈子。兩個小時後老人大汗淋漓，累到了骨子裡。不過圈子愈來愈小，從釣線的傾斜度他可以推斷出這條魚已經一邊游一邊不斷往上浮了。

老人眼前發黑已經有一個小時了，帶鹽味的汗水流進了眼睛，滲進了眼睛上方和額頭上的傷疤。他不擔心眼前發黑。拉釣線時他使足了勁，眼前發黑是很正常的。不過有兩次他覺得頭昏眼花，這倒讓他擔憂起來了。

「我可不能自暴自棄，就這麼死在一條魚面前，」他說，「既然我已經讓它乖乖地過來，天主呀，幫助我挺住吧。我會說一百遍《天主經》，一百遍《聖母經》。不過現在我可沒法說。」

"He is making the far part of his circle now," he said. I must hold all I can, he thought. The strain will shorten his circle each time. Perhaps in an hour I will see him. Now I must convince him and then I must kill him.

But the fish kept on circling slowly and the old man was wet with sweat and tired deep into his bones two hours later. But the circles were much shorter now and from the way the line slanted he could tell the fish had risen steadily while he swam.

For an hour the old man had been seeing black spots before his eyes and the sweat salted his eyes and salted the cut over his eye and on his forehead. He was not afraid of the black spots. They were normal at the tension that he was pulling on the line. Twice, though, he had felt faint and dizzy and that had worried him.

"I could not fail myself and die on a fish like this," he said. "Now that I have him coming so beautifully, God help me endure. I'll say a hundred Our Fathers and a hundred Hail Marys. But I cannot say them now."

權當已經說過了，他想。以後再補吧。

恰在這時，他雙手抓住的釣線猛地一撞一拉，來勢很猛，硬梆梆、沉甸甸的。

它在用矛一樣的嘴巴撞擊金屬接鉤繩，他想。這是必定會發生的，它不得不這樣做。不過這會讓它跳起來，我倒是情願它繼續打轉。為了呼吸空氣，它必須跳起來。但是每跳一次都會拉大魚鉤造成的傷口，最後它可能會脫鉤逃走。

「別跳了，魚呀，」他說，「別跳。」

這條魚又撞擊了金屬接鉤繩幾次，每次魚頭一撞，老人就送出一小段釣線。

我必須讓它在老地方痛，他想。我的疼痛沒有什麼大不了的，我能控制。但是它的疼痛會讓它發瘋。

Consider them said, he thought. I'll say them later.

Just then he felt a sudden banging and jerking on the line he held with his two hands. It was sharp and hard-feeling and heavy.

He is hitting the wire leader with his spear, he thought. That was bound to come. He had to do that. It may make him jump though and I would rather he stayed circling now. The jumps were necessary for him to take air. But after that each one can widen the opening of the hook wound and he can throw the hook.

"Don't jump, fish," he said. "Don't jump."

The fish hit the wire several times more and each time he shook his head the old man gave up a little line.

I must hold his pain where it is, he thought. Mine does not matter. I can control mine. But his pain could drive him mad.

過了一會兒，大魚不再撞擊金屬接鉤繩，又開始慢慢地打轉。現在老人正不斷地收回釣線。但是他又覺得頭暈了。他用左手舀起一點海水，淋在頭上。然後又淋了一點水，擦了擦頸背。

「我沒有抽筋，」他說，「它很快就會浮上來，不過我能堅持住。你必須得堅持住，這是不用說的了。」

他跪下來靠在船頭。暫時把釣線再次背在背上。現在，趁它轉遠的時候，我歇一歇吧，然後等它轉過來，我再站起來對付它，他決定了。

他很想在船頭歇一下，就讓魚轉了一個圈子，卻不往回收線。不過線的拉力說明大魚已經回頭朝小船游來。這時老人站了起來，開始轉動身子，雙手像織布一樣來回拉，收回了所有拉過來的釣線。

我從沒這麼累過，他想。現在颳起了貿易風，不過這有利於把它拉上來，我太需要這風了。

After a while the fish stopped beating at the wire and started circling slowly again. The old man was gaining line steadily now. But he felt faint again. He lifted some sea water with his left hand and put it on his head. Then he put more on and rubbed the back of his neck.

"I have no cramps," he said. "He'll be up soon and I can last. You have to last. Don't even speak of it."

He kneeled against the bow and, for a moment, slipped the line over his back again. I'll rest now while he goes out on the circle and then stand up and work on him when he comes in, he decided.

It was a great temptation to rest in the bow and let the fish make one circle by himself without recovering any line. But when the strain showed the fish had turned to come toward the boat, the old man rose to his feet and started the pivoting and the weaving pulling that brought in all the line he gained.

I'm tireder than I have ever been, he thought, and now the trade wind is rising. But that will be good to take him in with. I need that badly.

「等它下次朝外面轉圈的時候，我會歇一歇的。」他說，「我感覺好多了。那樣的話，再轉上兩、三圈，就能逮住它了。」

他的草帽戴得很靠腦後，他感覺到魚在轉身，結果釣線扯得他一屁股坐在了船頭。

魚呀，你忙吧，他想。你轉身時我再收拾你。

海浪大了許多。不過吹的是預示晴天的風，他需要這種風送他回家。

「船只要朝西南方向開就行了，」他說，「男子漢從不會在海上迷路，況且這不過是個長長的島嶼[18]。」

魚在轉第三圈的時候，他第一次看到它了。

18 指古巴的地形像一個島。

"I'll rest on the next turn as he goes out," he said. "I feel much better. Then in two or three turns more I will have him."

His straw hat was far on the back of his head and he sank down into the bow with the pull of the line as he felt the fish turn.

You work now, fish, he thought. I'll take you at the turn.

The sea had risen considerably. But it was a fair-weather breeze and he had to have it to get home.

"I'll just steer south and west," he said. "A man is never lost at sea and it is a long island."

It was on the third turn that he saw the fish first.

他先看到的是一個黑色的影子，那影子費了好久才鑽出小船，他簡直難以相信魚身會那麼長。

「不，」他說，「它不可能有那麼大。」

但是它就是有那麼大，轉了這一圈以後，它浮出了水面，與他相距只有三十碼。老人看到魚尾露出水面，比一把大鐮刀的刀刃還要長，在深藍色的海面上呈淡紫色。魚尾巴往後倒，掠過海水。魚在海面上游的時候，老人能看見巨大的魚身以及上面紫色的帶狀條紋。魚的背鰭朝下，巨大的胸鰭張得很大。

魚轉這一圈時，老人能看見魚眼睛，還有兩條鯽魚在它旁邊游著。它們時而貼近它，時而逃竄開，時而又悠閒地在它的影子裡游弋。兩條魚每條都不止三英尺長，游得快時像鰻魚一樣甩動著整個身子。

He saw him first as a dark shadow that took so long to pass under the boat that he could not believe its length.

"No," he said. "He can't be that big."

But he was that big and at the end of this circle he came to the surface only thirty yards away and the man saw his tail out of water. It was higher than a big scythe blade and a very pale lavender above the dark blue water. It raked back and as the fish swam just below the surface the old man could see his huge bulk and the purple stripes that banded him. His dorsal fin was down and his huge pectorals were spread wide.

On this circle the old man could see the fish's eye and the two gray sucking fish that swam around him. Sometimes they attached themselves to him. Sometimes they darted off. Sometimes they would swim easily in his shadow. They were each over three feet long and when they swam fast they lashed their whole bodies like eels.

現在老人在冒汗，除了因為太陽，還有別的原因。每逢大魚平靜地轉身，老人都會收回釣線。他肯定，再轉兩圈，他就有機會把魚叉插進魚身了。

但我必須把它拉得靠近，靠近，再靠近，他想。魚叉千萬別插在頭部，而必須插進心臟。

「鎮靜些，用足力氣，老頭兒。」他說。

在接下來的打轉中，大魚已經露出背來，但離船還是遠了一些。再接下來打轉時，它離船仍舊太遠，但出水更多了。老人確信再收回一些釣線，他就可以把它拉到船邊。

他早就準備好了魚叉，叉上的那卷輕繩放在一個圓形籃子裡，繩的另一頭繫在船頭的纜樁上。

The old man was sweating now but from something else besides the sun. On each calm placid turn the fish made he was gaining line and he was sure that in two turns more he would have a chance to get the harpoon in.

But I must get him close, close, close, he thought. I mustn't try for the head. I must get the heart.

"Be calm and strong, old man," he said.

On the next circle the fish's back was out but he was a little too far from the boat. On the next circle he was still too far away but he was higher out of water and the old man was sure that by gaining some more line he could have him alongside.

He had rigged his harpoon long before and its coil of light rope was in a round basket and the end was made fast to the bitt in the bow.

大魚打著轉靠近了，這時它很沉著，看上去很漂亮，只有大尾巴還在划動。老人用盡力氣把它拉得靠近些。一剎那間，大魚往側面斜了一下，隨後豎直身子，又開始打起轉來。

「我拉動它了，」老人說，「我拉動它了。」

他再次感到頭暈，但還是使出渾身力氣拉住大魚。我把它拉動了，他想。也許這回就能把它拉過來了。拉呀，手，他想。撐住呀，腿。幫忙堅持一下，腦袋。幫忙堅持一下。你從來沒有暈倒過。這回我就要把它拉過來了。

但是大魚還沒有靠近，他就使出渾身勁兒拚力拉釣線，大魚被拉得側了過來，但隨之又豎直身子，游走了。

「魚呀，」老人說，「魚呀，反正你是死定了。難道你要把我也弄死？」

The fish was coming in on his circle now calm and beautiful looking and only his great tail moving. The old man pulled on him all that he could to bring him closer. For just a moment the fish turned a little on his side. Then he straightened himself and began another circle.

"I moved him," the old man said. "I moved him then."

He felt faint again now but he held on the great fish all the strain that he could. I moved him, he thought. Maybe this time I can get him over. Pull, hands, he thought. Hold up, legs. Last for me, head. Last for me. You never went. This time I'll pull him over.

But when he put all of his effort on, starting it well out before the fish came alongside and pulling with all his strength, the fish pulled part way over and then righted himself and swam away.

"Fish," the old man said. "Fish, you are going to have to die anyway. Do you have to kill me too?"

那樣的話，我就會一無所獲了，他想。他的嘴巴乾得說不出話來，卻又搆不到水。這回我必須把它拉到旁邊來，他想。我撐不了幾圈了。是的，你行，他對自己說，你永遠都行。

下一次轉圈時，他差點把它逮住了。可是大魚又豎直身子，慢慢地游走了。

你要弄死我，魚，老人想。不過你有權這樣做。我還從來沒有見過比你更大、更漂亮，或者更沉著、更高尚的東西，兄弟。來吧，把我弄死吧，我不在乎是誰殺了誰。

現在你腦子迷糊了，他想。你得保持頭腦清醒。你得保持頭腦清醒，知道如何像男子漢那樣吃苦，或者像魚一樣，他想。

「清醒些，腦袋，」他說，聲音輕得幾乎聽不見，「清醒些。」

That way nothing is accomplished, he thought. His mouth was too dry to speak but he could not reach for the water now. I must get him alongside this time, he thought. I am not good for many more turns. Yes you are, he told himself. You're good for ever.

On the next turn, he nearly had him. But again the fish righted himself and swam slowly away.

You are killing me, fish, the old man thought. But you have a right to. Never have I seen a greater, or more beautiful, or a calmer or more noble thing than you, brother. Come on and kill me. I do not care who kills who.

Now you are getting confused in the head, he thought. You must keep your head clear. Keep your head clear and know how to suffer like a man. Or a fish, he thought.

"Clear up, head," he said in a voice he could hardly hear. "Clear up."

魚又轉了兩圈，還是老樣子。

我不知道這是怎麼回事，老人想。每次他都覺得自己差不多要昏倒了。我不知道這是怎麼回事，但我會再試一次。

他又試了一次，把魚拉得斜過來的時候，他又覺得自己就要昏過去。魚豎直身子，又慢慢地游走了，巨大的尾巴在海面上搖搖晃晃地前進。

我會再試一下，老人許諾說，儘管這時他的雙手已經軟弱無力，眼睛只能一陣陣看清東西。

他又試了一下，結果還是老樣子。就這樣了，他想，他覺得還沒動手他就已經要昏過去了。我要再試一次。

Twice more it was the same on the turns.

I do not know, the old man thought. He had been on the point of feeling himself go each time. I do not know. But I will try it once more.

He tried it once more and he felt himself going when he turned the fish. The fish righted himself and swam off again slowly with the great tail weaving in the air.

I'll try it again, the old man promised, although his hands were mushy now and he could only see well in flashes.

He tried it again and it was the same. So he thought, and he felt himself going before he started; I will try it once again.

他忍受著一切痛苦，拿出餘下的力氣和早已喪失的自尊來對付魚的痛苦掙扎。魚朝他身邊游過來，在一旁溫順地游著，魚嘴幾乎碰到了小船的船殼外板。魚開始從小船旁游過，身子又長又寬，入水很深，銀光閃閃，布滿紫色條紋。在水裡，魚身顯得長不可測。

老人丟下釣線，一隻腳踩在上面，把魚叉舉得盡可能地高，用足力氣，加上剛剛鼓起的勁兒往下刺去，刺進了大胸鰭後面的背部，那胸鰭聳起在空中，跟老人的胸部一般高。他感覺到鐵尖已經插進去，便倚在魚叉上，藉著渾身的重量，把魚叉又往裡插。

隨後，魚又活蹦亂跳起來，儘管已是必死無疑。它高高躍出水面，展示了它巨大的長度和寬度以及所有的力和美。它似乎懸在半空，就在船中老人的頭上。接著，它啪啦一聲掉進水裡，濺起水沫，落在老人的身上和整條船上。

He took all his pain and what was left of his strength and his long gone pride and he put it against the fish's agony and the fish came over onto his side and swam gently on his side, his bill almost touching the planking of the skiff and started to pass the boat, long, deep, wide, silver and barred with purple and interminable in the water.

The old man dropped the line and put his foot on it and lifted the harpoon as high as he could and drove it down with all his strength, and more strength he had just summoned, into the fish's side just behind the great chest fin that rose high in the air to the altitude of the man's chest. He felt the iron go in and he leaned on it and drove it further and then pushed all his weight after it.

Then the fish came alive, with his death in him, and rose high out of the water showing all his great length and width and all his power and his beauty. He seemed to hang in the air above the old man in the skiff. Then he fell into the water with a crash that sent spray over the old man and over all of the skiff.

老人覺得昏眩，噁心，看不清東西。但還是放出了魚叉線，讓它慢慢地從擦破了皮的手中送出去。待眼睛管用時，他看見魚已經背朝下，銀白色肚皮向上翻了。魚叉柄從魚的肩部斜伸出來。魚的心臟裡流出鮮紅的血，使海水變了色。開始是暗黑色，像一英里多深的藍色海水裡的魚群。然後像一朵雲那麼擴散開去。魚呈銀白色，一動不動，隨海浪漂浮著。

老人在眼睛好使的那一剎那仔細地瞧著。然後，他把魚叉繩在船頭的纜樁上繞了兩圈，將腦袋靠在手上。

「保持頭腦清醒，」他靠在船頭的木板上說，「我是個累得不行的老人。但我已經殺死了這條魚，它是我的兄弟。現在我得幹苦活了。」

The old man felt faint and sick and he could not see well. But he cleared the harpoon line and let it run slowly through his raw hands and, when he could see, he saw the fish was on his back with his silver belly up. The shaft of the harpoon was projecting at an angle from the fish's shoulder and the sea was discolouring with the red of the blood from his heart. First it was dark as a shoal in the blue water that was more than a mile deep. Then it spread like a cloud. The fish was silvery and still and floated with the waves.

The old man looked carefully in the glimpse of vision that he had. Then he took two turns of the harpoon line around the bitt in the bow and laid his head on his hands.

"Keep my head clear," he said against the wood of the bow. "I am a tired old man. But I have killed this fish which is my brother and now I must do the slave work."

現在我得準備繩套和繩索，把它綁在船旁邊，他想。即使我們有兩個人，往小船裡灌滿水把魚放進去，再把船裡的水舀乾，這條小船也絕對裝不下它。我得把一切都準備好，把它拉近、捆綁好，再豎起桅杆、撐起帆回家。

他開始把魚拉近到他身邊，以便把一根繩索塞進魚鰓，從嘴裡穿出來，把魚頭綁在船頭邊。我要瞧瞧它，他想，我要碰碰它，摸摸它。它是我的財富，他想。但是這不是我想摸它的原因。我想我摸到了它的心，他想，就在我第二次把魚叉扎進去的時候。現在我要把它拉近，拴住，用一個繩套縛住尾巴，另一個繩套捆住魚身中部，將它綁在小船上。

「動手吧，老頭兒，」他說著喝了一小口水，「現在搏鬥已經結束，但還有很多苦活要幹。」

Now I must prepare the nooses and the rope to lash him alongside, he thought. Even if we were two and swamped her to load him and bailed her out, this skiff would never hold him. I must prepare everything, then bring him in and lash him well and step the mast and set sail for home.

He started to pull the fish in to have him alongside so that he could pass a line through his gills and out his mouth and make his head fast alongside the bow. I want to see him, he thought, and to touch and to feel him. He is my fortune, he thought. But that is not why I wish to feel him. I think I felt his heart, he thought. When I pushed on the harpoon shaft the second time. Bring him in now and make him fast and get the noose around his tail and another around his middle to bind him to the skiff.

"Get to work, old man," he said. He took a very small drink of the water. "There is very much slave work to be done now that the fight is over."

他仰望天空，接著又看了看船外的魚。他仔細瞧著太陽。現在才剛過正午，他想。貿易風起來了。釣線已經毫無用處。到了家，孩子和我會把它們捻接起來的。

「過來吧，魚。」他說。但是魚沒有過來，卻躺在海水裡，翻滾著。老人將小船朝它靠過去。

待他和魚並排，魚頭靠著船頭時，他簡直難以相信這條魚會那麼大。他把魚叉上的繩索從纜樁上解下，穿過魚鰓，從嘴裡拉出來，在魚嘴上繞了一圈，穿過另外一邊魚鰓，又在魚嘴上繞了一圈，將這兩股繩打成一個結，繫在船頭的纜樁上。他割下一段繩子，到船尾用繩套縛住魚尾巴。這條魚已經從原先的紫色和銀色轉為了純粹的銀色，魚身上的條紋露出尾巴一樣的淡紫色。這些條紋比男人張開手指的手還要寬，魚眼睛看上去像潛望鏡裡的鏡片或是遊行隊伍裡的聖徒那樣冷漠。

He looked up at the sky and then out to his fish. He looked at the sun carefully. It is not much more than noon, he thought. And the trade wind is rising. The lines all mean nothing now. The boy and I will splice them when we are home.

"Come on, fish," he said. But the fish did not come. Instead he lay there wallowing now in the seas and the old man pulled the skiff up onto him.

When he was even with him and had the fish's head against the bow he could not believe his size. But he untied the harpoon rope from the bitt, passed it through the fish's gills and out his jaws, made a turn around his sword then passed the rope through the other gill, made another turn around the bill and knotted the double rope and made it fast to the bitt in the bow. He cut the rope then and went astern to noose the tail. The fish had turned silver from his original purple and silver, and the stripes showed the same pale violet colour as his tail. They were wider than a man's hand with his fingers spread and the fish's eye looked as detached as the mirrors in a periscope or as a saint in a procession.

「要宰殺它，只有用這個辦法。」老人說。喝了水後，他感覺好些了。他知道自己不會暈過去了，他的頭腦是清楚的。看樣子它會超過一千五百磅，他想。也許還要多得多。如果它開膛洗淨後的重量還剩下三分之二，按三毛錢一磅算，一共該是多少錢呢？

「我需要用鉛筆來算算，」他說，「我的腦袋還沒那麼清楚。不過我想名將迪馬喬今天會為我感到自豪。我沒長骨刺，但手和背痛得厲害。」不知道骨刺是什麼，他想。也許我們長了骨刺卻並不知道。

他把魚綁在船頭、船尾和船中間的横坐板上。這條魚那麼大，彷彿是在小船旁邊捆綁了一條大得多的船。他割下一截繩子，把魚的下巴在魚嘴上縛緊，免得嘴巴張開，行起船來好盡可能利索些。接著，他豎起桅杆，撐起那根用做手鉤的木棒和吊杆，張開打了補丁的風帆，小船便起航了。他半躺在船尾，朝西南方向駛去。

"It was the only way to kill him," the old man said. He was feeling better since the water and he knew he would not go away and his head was clear. He's over fifteen hundred pounds the way he is, he thought. Maybe much more. If he dresses out two-thirds of that at thirty cents a pound?

"I need a pencil for that," he said. "My head is not that clear. But I think the great DiMaggio would be proud of me today. I had no bone spurs. But the hands and the back hurt truly." I wonder what a bone spur is, he thought. Maybe we have them without knowing of it.

He made the fish fast to bow and stern and to the middle thwart. He was so big it was like lashing a much bigger skiff alongside. He cut a piece of line and tied the fish's lower jaw against his bill so his mouth would not open and they would sail as cleanly as possible. Then he stepped the mast and, with the stick that was his gaff and with his boom rigged, the patched sail drew, the boat began to move, and half lying in the stern he sailed south-west.

他不需要指南針來辨別西南方向。他只要感覺一下貿易風和帆的飄向就行了。我還是放出一根帶勺形假餌的細線，設法搞點吃的，潤一潤喉嚨。但他找不到勺形假餌，而沙丁魚都已經爛掉了。於是經過一簇黃色馬尾藻時，他就用手鉤把它鉤了上來，抖了抖，裡面的小蝦都落到了船殼外板上，總有十多隻，都像盲潛蚤那樣活蹦亂跳。老人用大拇指和食指把蝦頭掐了就吃，連同蝦殼和尾巴都嚼了下去。蝦很小，但他知道它們有營養而且味道也不錯。

He did not need a compass to tell him where south-west was. He only needed the feel of the trade wind and the drawing of the sail. I better put a small line out with a spoon on it and try and get something to eat and drink for the moisture. But he could not find a spoon and his sardines were rotten. So he hooked a patch of yellow gulf weed with the gaff as they passed and shook it so that the small shrimps that were in it fell onto the planking of the skiff. There were more than a dozen of them and they jumped and kicked like sand fleas. The old man pinched their heads off with his thumb and forefinger and ate them chewing up the shells and the tails. They were very tiny but he knew they were nourishing and they tasted good.

老人的瓶裡還有兩口水，吃完蝦後他喝了半口。考慮到現有的障礙，船已經行駛得不錯了，他把胳膊擱在舵柄上駕駛著。他能看到那條魚，只要瞧一瞧自己的手，感覺到背靠在船尾，就知道這是確確實實的事，不是夢。有一度，他感覺很不好，覺得快要完蛋了，他想這也許是一場夢。後來，他看到魚躍出水面，一動不動地懸在半空中然後才落下來，他敢肯定這很有些奇妙，令他難以相信。隨後，他的眼睛就看不清了，儘管現在視力已跟往常一樣了。

The old man still had two drinks of water in the bottle and he used half of one after he had eaten the shrimps. The skiff was sailing well considering the handicaps and he steered with the tiller under his arm. He could see the fish and he had only to look at his hands and feel his back against the stern to know that this had truly happened and was not a dream. At one time when he was feeling so badly toward the end, he had thought perhaps it was a dream. Then when he had seen the fish come out of the water and hang motionless in the sky before he fell, he was sure there was some great strangeness and he could not believe it. Then he could not see well, although now he saw as well as ever.

現在，他知道魚已經到手，他的手和背也不是夢。手恢復得很快，他想。我讓手裡的血放光了，鹽水能治癒它們。真正的海灣深色水是世上最好的良藥。我所要做的就是保持頭腦清醒。雙手已經盡職了，小船也行駛得很好。魚嘴閉著，魚尾直上直下地擺動，我們像兄弟一樣行駛著。後來，他的腦袋有點迷糊了，他想是魚帶我回家，還是我帶著魚回家呢？要是我將它拖在船後，那就不存在這個問題了。或者，要是魚在小船裡，失去了一切尊嚴，那也不會有問題了。但是，他們並排綁著，一起往前駛去。老人想，要是這讓它高興，就算是它帶我回家吧。我不過是用了詭計才比它強，而且它並不想傷害我。

Now he knew there was the fish and his hands and back were no dream. The hands cure quickly, he thought. I bled them clean and the salt water will heal them. The dark water of the true gulf is the greatest healer that there is. All I must do is keep the head clear. The hands have done their work and we sail well. With his mouth shut and his tail straight up and down we sail like brothers. Then his head started to become a little unclear and he thought, is he bringing me in or am I bringing him in? If I were towing him behind there would be no question. Nor if the fish were in the skiff, with all dignity gone, there would be no question either. But they were sailing together lashed side by side and the old man thought, let him bring me in if it pleases him. I am only better than him through trickery and he meant me no harm.

他們行駛得很順利。老人把雙手浸在鹽水裡，並竭力保持頭腦清醒。高高的天空中飄著積雲，上方有很多卷雲，由此老人知道整個晚上都會有風。老人不時去瞧那條魚，以肯定這是真的。一個小時之後，第一條鯊魚襲擊了這條大魚。

鯊魚的來襲並不偶然。它是從深水裡游上來的，因為黑雲狀的魚血沉積下來，散布在一英里深的海裡。鯊魚上來得那麼快，毫無預兆地劃破藍色的海水，出現在太陽底下。隨後，它又回到水裡，捕捉到血腥味，開始順著小船和魚的航道游來。

They sailed well and the old man soaked his hands in the salt water and tried to keep his head clear. There were high cumulus clouds and enough cirrus above them so that the old man knew the breeze would last all night. The old man looked at the fish constantly to make sure it was true. It was an hour before the first shark hit him.

The shark was not an accident. He had come up from deep down in the water as the dark cloud of blood had settled and dispersed in the mile deep sea. He had come up so fast and absolutely without caution that he broke the surface of the blue water and was in the sun. Then he fell back into the sea and picked up the scent and started swimming on the course the skiff and the fish had taken.

有時候，鯊魚會找不到氣味，但又會重新捕捉到它，也許不過是蛛絲馬跡，鯊魚卻會游得很快，緊追上去。這是一條很大的灰鯖鮫，生來游得跟海裡最快的魚一樣快。除了魚嘴，渾身都很漂亮。它的背像劍魚的背那麼藍，肚皮為銀色，魚皮光滑漂亮。它的體態像劍魚，就是那張大嘴不一樣。這時它嘴巴緊閉，貼著水面游得很快，高高的背鰭刀子一般在水裡穿行，毫不抖動。在緊閉的雙唇裡，八排牙齒向內傾斜。這不是大多數鯊魚常見的金字塔形牙齒，樣子倒像捲成爪子模樣的人的手指。它的牙齒跟老人的手指差不多長，兩側有著像剃刀般鋒利的刀口。這種魚生來就是捕食海裡所有魚的，速度那麼快，體格那麼強壯，又是全副武裝，所以沒有其他敵人。現在，它聞到了新鮮的血腥味，便開始加速，藍色的背鰭劃破了海水。

Sometimes he lost the scent. But he would pick it up again, or have just a trace of it, and he swam fast and hard on the course. He was a very big Mako shark built to swim as fast as the fastest fish in the sea and everything about him was beautiful except his jaws. His back was as blue as a sword fish's and his belly was silver and his hide was smooth and handsome. He was built as a sword fish except for his huge jaws which were tight shut now as he swam fast, just under the surface with his high dorsal fin knifing through the water without wavering. Inside the closed double lip of his jaws all of his eight rows of teeth were slanted inwards. They were not the ordinary pyramid-shaped teeth of most sharks. They were shaped like a man's fingers when they are crisped like claws. They were nearly as long as the fingers of the old man and they had razor-sharp cutting edges on both sides. This was a fish built to feed on all the fishes in the sea, that were so fast and strong and well armed that they had no other enemy. Now he speeded up as he smelled the fresher scent and his blue dorsal fin cut the water.

老人看著鯊魚過來，知道它天不怕地不怕，想幹什麼就幹什麼。他一邊看著鯊魚靠近，一面準備好魚叉，把繩子繫緊了。可是繩子太短，缺了一截，就是割下來捆魚的那一截。

老人腦子清醒好使，決心很大，卻不抱什麼希望。好景不長，他想。瞧著鯊魚逼近，他看了看那條大魚。也許這只是一場夢，他想。我不可能阻止它攻擊我，但也許我能逮住它。登土鯊[19]，他想。算你媽倒楣。

19 原文為西班牙語，此處為音譯，用於稱呼灰鯖鮫。

When the old man saw him coming he knew that this was a shark that had no fear at all and would do exactly what he wished. He prepared the harpoon and made the rope fast while he watched the shark come on. The rope was short as it lacked what he had cut away to lash the fish.

The old man's head was clear and good now and he was full of resolution but he had little hope. It was too good to last, he thought. He took one look at the great fish as he watched the shark close in. It might as well have been a dream, he thought. I cannot keep him from hitting me but maybe I can get him. *Dentuso*, he thought. Bad luck to your mother.

鯊魚快速靠近船尾，在襲擊大魚的時候，老人見它張開大嘴，眼睛怪怪的，牙齒嗞嚓一聲插進魚尾上方的魚肉。鯊魚的頭鑽出水面，背也露了出來，老人聽見鯊魚撕開大魚皮肉的聲音，他把魚叉猛地往下刺向鯊魚頭部，插進兩眼之間那條線與從鼻子筆直往後的那條線的交點上。其實那些線是不存在的。只有厚重尖利的藍色腦袋，巨大的眼睛，嗞嚓作響、吞噬一切的攻擊性的嘴巴。不過那是魚腦所在，老人刺中了這個地方。他用血汁模糊的雙手使出全身力氣，把魚叉結結實實地刺了進去。他刺的時候不抱希望，卻帶著決心和十足的惡意。

The shark closed fast astern and when he hit the fish the old man saw his mouth open and his strange eyes and the clicking chop of the teeth as he drove forward in the meat just above the tail. The shark's head was out of water and his back was coming out and the old man could hear the noise of skin and flesh ripping on the big fish when he rammed the harpoon down onto the shark's head at a spot where the line between his eyes intersected with the line that ran straight back from his nose. There were no such lines. There was only the heavy sharp blue head and the big eyes and the clicking, thrusting all-swallowing jaws. But that was the location of the brain and the old man hit it. He hit it with his blood mushed hands driving a good harpoon with all his strength. He hit it without hope but with resolution and complete malignancy.

鯊魚翻過身來，老人看見它的眼睛已沒有了生氣。隨後鯊魚又翻了個身，身上裹了兩圈繩索。老人知道鯊魚已經死了，但它不願接受死亡。接著，鯊魚肚皮朝天，甩動著尾巴，咯咯地咬著嘴巴，像一艘快艇似的破浪前進。尾巴擊水的地方泛起了白色的水花，繩索繃緊了，顫抖著，最後斷掉。這時，鯊魚四分之三的身體完全露出水面，在那兒靜靜地躺了一會兒，老人瞧著它。隨後，鯊魚慢慢地下沉。

「它叼走了近四十磅肉。」老人大聲說。還帶走了我的魚叉和全部的繩索，他想。現在我的大魚又在淌血了，而且還會有其他鯊魚來襲。

大魚被咬得不成樣子，他不想再去看它。魚受到襲擊時，就彷彿他自己受到了襲擊。

The shark swung over and the old man saw his eye was not alive and then he swung over once again, wrapping himself in two loops of the rope. The old man knew that he was dead but the shark would not accept it. Then, on his back, with his tail lashing and his jaws clicking, the shark plowed over the water as a speed-boat does. The water was white where his tail beat it and three-quarters of his body was clear above the water when the rope came taut, shivered, and then snapped. The shark lay quietly for a little while on the surface and the old man watched him. Then he went down very slowly.

"He took about forty pounds," the old man said aloud. He took my harpoon too and all the rope, he thought, and now my fish bleeds again and there will be others.

He did not like to look at the fish anymore since he had been mutilated. When the fish had been hit it was as though he himself were hit.

不過，攻擊我那條魚的鯊魚被我給宰了，他想。我見到過的登士鯊就數它最大。天主知道，我是見過大鯊魚的。

好景不長，他想。我現在真希望這是一場夢，希望我根本沒有釣到過這條魚，希望獨個兒在床上躺在報紙上。

「但是人不是為失敗而生的，」他說，「一個人可以被毀滅，卻不能被打敗。」不過我還是很難過，我竟宰了這條魚，他想。現在困難的時刻就要來臨，而我連魚叉也沒有了。登士鯊血腥、有能力、強壯、聰明。不過我比它還聰明。也許不是這樣，他想。也許只不過是我比它武裝得更好而已。

「別想了，老頭兒，」他大聲說，「順著這條航線走吧，事情來了再應付。」

But I killed the shark that hit my fish, he thought. And he was the biggest *dentuso* that I have ever seen. And God knows that I have seen big ones.

It was too good to last, he thought. I wish it had been a dream now and that I had never hooked the fish and was alone in bed on the newspapers.

"But man is not made for defeat," he said. "A man can be destroyed but not defeated." I am sorry that I killed the fish though, he thought. Now the bad time is coming and I do not even have the harpoon. The *dentuso* is cruel and able and strong and intelligent. But I was more intelligent than he was. Perhaps not, he thought. Perhaps I was only better armed.

"Don't think, old man," he said aloud. "Sail on this course and take it when it comes."

但是我必須要考慮。因為我只剩下這麼點事兒了，這件事和棒球賽。我刺進了它的腦袋，不知道名將迪馬喬會怎麼想。這沒有什麼了不起，他想。誰都能做到。但是，你認為我雙手造成的麻煩，會像骨刺那麼大嗎？我無法知道。我的腳後跟從來沒有出過事，除了有一次，游泳時被踩著的一條魟魚刺了一下，下半條腿麻木了，疼得無法忍受。

「想些開心的事兒，老頭兒，」他說，「現在，你每過一分鐘就離家更近一點。少了四十磅，船行駛起來就更輕鬆了。」

他心裡很明白進了水流深處會發生什麼事情。但現在是沒有辦法可想了。

「不對，有辦法，」他大聲說，「我可以把刀綁在船槳柄上。」

他用胳膊夾著舵柄，腳踩著帆腳索，把這件事做了。

But I must think, he thought. Because it is all I have left. That and baseball. I wonder how the great DiMaggio would have liked the way I hit him in the brain? It was no great thing, he thought. Any man could do it. But do you think my hands were as great a handicap as the bone spurs? I cannot know. I never had anything wrong with my heel except the time the sting ray stung it when I stepped on him when swimming and paralyzed the lower leg and made the unbearable pain.

"Think about something cheerful, old man," he said. "Every minute now you are closer to home. You sail lighter for the loss of forty pounds."

He knew quite well the pattern of what could happen when he reached the inner part of the current. But there was nothing to be done now.

"Yes there is," he said aloud. "I can lash my knife to the butt of one of the oars."

So he did that with the tiller under his arm and the sheet of the sail under his foot.

「現在，」他說，「我雖然還是個老頭兒，但並不是手無寸鐵的。」

這時微風吹來，船走得很順。他只看著魚的前半段，恢復了一些希望。

人不抱希望是很傻的，他想。另外，我相信這是罪過。別去想罪過了，他想。現在，沒有罪過已經夠麻煩了。而且，我又不懂什麼是罪過。

我不懂這東西，也說不準是不是相信這東西。也許殺了這條魚就是罪過。我猜想是的，即使我這麼做是為了養活自己，為了讓很多人有魚吃。但那樣的話，幹什麼都是罪過。別想罪過了。就是要想，也已經太晚了，何況有人是受雇來考慮罪過的。就讓他們去思考吧。就像魚生來是魚那樣，你生來就是個漁夫。聖彼得[20]是個漁夫，就像名將迪馬喬的父親是個漁夫一樣。

20 耶穌剛開始傳道時在加利利海邊所收的四個門徒之一。

"Now," he said. "I am still an old man. But I am not unarmed."

The breeze was fresh now and he sailed on well. He watched only the forward part of the fish and some of his hope returned.

It is silly not to hope, he thought. Besides I believe it is a sin. Do not think about sin, he thought. There are enough problems now without sin. Also I have no understanding of it.

I have no understanding of it and I am not sure that I believe in it. Perhaps it was a sin to kill the fish. I suppose it was even though I did it to keep me alive and feed many people. But then everything is a sin. Do not think about sin. It is much too late for that and there are people who are paid to do it. Let them think about it. You were born to be a fisherman as the fish was born to be a fish. San Pedro was a fisherman as was the father of the great DiMaggio.

不過，他喜歡考慮自己捲入的一切事情。既然沒有書讀，又沒有收音機聽，他便想了很多，而且繼續想著罪過的問題。你把魚殺了，不光是為了活命和賣給人家當食品，他想。你殺它是出於自尊，因為你是個漁夫。它活著的時候你喜歡它，死了你還是喜歡。要是你喜歡它，殺了它就不是罪過。要不，會不會是更大的罪過？

「你想得太多了，老頭兒。」他大聲說。

但是，你享受殺死登土鯊的樂趣，他想。它同你一樣，以活魚為生。它不是食腐動物，也不像某些鯊魚那樣只是個活動飯袋。它漂亮、高尚、無所畏懼。

「我出於自衛殺了它，」老人大聲說，「而且殺得乾淨俐落。」

But he liked to think about all things that he was involved in and since there was nothing to read and he did not have a radio, he thought much and he kept on thinking about sin. You did not kill the fish only to keep alive and to sell for food, he thought. You killed him for pride and because you are a fisherman. You loved him when he was alive and you loved him after. If you love him, it is not a sin to kill him. Or is it more?

"You think too much, old man," he said aloud.

But you enjoyed killing the *dentuso*, he thought. He lives on the live fish as you do. He is not a scavenger nor just a moving appetite as some sharks are. He is beautiful and noble and knows no fear of anything.

"I killed him in self-defense," the old man said aloud. "And I killed him well."

另外，他想，某種意義上說，是一物殺一物。捕魚能要我的命，也能讓我活著。那孩子讓我活著，他想。我決不能太自欺欺人。

他靠在船邊，從被鯊魚咬過的魚身上撕下一塊肉。他咀嚼著，發現肉質很好，味道鮮美，像豬肉一樣，肉很緊，汁水多，但色不紅。魚肉裡沒有什麼筋，在市場上能賣出最高價。但就是沒法去除魚在水裡留下的血腥味。老人知道，大難就要臨頭了。

風不斷地吹著，稍稍逆轉為東北方向，他知道那意味著風勢不會減弱。老人往前望去，卻看不見任何船帆，也不見船身，或者從船上冒出的煙。只看見飛魚從船頭躍起，滑向兩邊，還有一簇簇黃色的馬尾藻。他甚至連一隻鳥都看不到。

Besides, he thought, everything kills everything else in some way. Fishing kills me exactly as it keeps me alive. The boy keeps me alive, he thought. I must not deceive myself too much.

He leaned over the side and pulled loose a piece of the meat of the fish where the shark had cut him. He chewed it and noted its quality and its good taste. It was firm and juicy, like meat, but it was not red. There was no stringiness in it and he knew that it would bring the highest price in the market. But there was no way to keep its scent out of the water and the old man knew that a very bad time was coming.

The breeze was steady. It had backed a little further into the north-east and he knew that meant that it would not fall off. The old man looked ahead of him but he could see no sails nor could he see the hull nor the smoke of any ship. There were only the flying fish that went up from his bow sailing away to either side and the yellow patches of gulf-weed. He could not even see a bird.

他一邊駕著船走了兩個小時，一邊在船尾歇息，有時嚼一點旗魚肉，養精蓄銳，這時他看到了兩條鯊魚中的第一條。

「Ay。」他大聲說。這是個無法翻譯的字眼，也許不過是一個人覺得釘子穿過手，釘進了木頭，不由自主發出的一種聲音。

「加拉諾鯊[21]。」他大聲說。他看見第二個鰭緊跟著第一個出現了，從褐色的三角形的鰭和尾巴大幅度擺動的樣子，他認出這是六鰓鯊。這兩條鯊魚聞到了血腥味，激動不已，卻因為餓傻了，激動中忽而迷失，忽而又找到了血腥味。但是它們一直在靠近小船。

21 原文為西班牙語，此處為音譯，用於稱呼六鰓鯊。

He had sailed for two hours, resting in the stern and sometimes chewing a bit of the meat from the marlin, trying to rest and to be strong, when he saw the first of the two sharks.

"*Ay*," he said aloud. There is no translation for this word and perhaps it is just a noise such as a man might make, involuntarily, feeling the nail go through his hands and into the wood.

"*Galanos*," he said aloud. He had seen the second fin now coming up behind the first and had identified them as shovel-nosed sharks by the brown, triangular fin and the sweeping movements of the tail. They had the scent and were excited and in the stupidity of their great hunger they were losing and finding the scent in their excitement. But they were closing all the time.

老人繫好帆腳索，卡住舵柄。隨後拿起綁著刀子的船槳，盡可能輕地舉了起來，因為雙手已疼得不聽使喚了。接著，他張開手，輕輕地握住船槳，讓雙手鬆弛下來。他一邊握緊雙手，使它們忍住疼痛而不畏縮，一邊看著鯊魚過來。現在，他看得見鯊魚那又寬又扁鏟子一般尖利的頭了，還有那頂端是白色的寬闊胸鰭。這是兩隻可惡的鯊魚，是臭烘烘的食腐動物，也是殺手，它們一旦餓慌了連槳和舵都會咬。就是這種鯊魚會在海龜熟睡在水面上時，咬掉它們的腿和鰭狀肢。要是餓了，它們甚至會攻擊人，即使人身上沒有魚的血腥味和魚的黏液。

「Ay，」老人說，「加拉諾鯊，來吧，加拉諾鯊。」

The old man made the sheet fast and jammed the tiller. Then he took up the oar with the knife lashed to it. He lifted it as lightly as he could because his hands rebelled at the pain. Then he opened and closed them on it lightly to loosen them. He closed them firmly so they would take the pain now and would not flinch and watched the sharks come. He could see their wide, flattened, shovel-pointed heads now and their white-tipped wide pectoral fins. They were hateful sharks, bad smelling, scavengers as well as killers and when they were hungry they would bite at an oar or the rudder of a boat. It was these sharks that would cut the turtles' legs and flippers off when the turtles were asleep on the surface, and they would hit a man in the water, if they were hungry, even if the man had no smell of fish blood nor of fish slime on him.

"*Ay*," the old man said. "*Galanos*. Come on *Galanos*."

它們來了，但過來的方式和灰鯖鮫不同。其中一條打了個彎，鑽到小船底下，不見了蹤影。老人能感覺到小船在搖晃，原來鯊魚在撕拉著大魚。另外一條鯊魚張著細長的黃眼睛，瞧著老人。隨後它飛快地游過來，張開半圓形的大嘴，朝著魚被咬過的地方咬下去。鯊魚褐色的頭頂以及腦袋與脊髓相接的背部，露出一道清晰的條紋。老人把綁在槳上的刀往那個交叉點刺去，再拔出來，又刺進鯊魚貓眼一樣的黃色眼睛裡。鯊魚放下大魚，往水下溜，臨死前吞食了咬走的魚肉。

They came. But they did not come as the Mako had come. One turned and went out of sight under the skiff and the old man could feel the skiff shake as he jerked and pulled on the fish. The other watched the old man with his slitted yellow eyes and then came in fast with his half circle of jaws wide to hit the fish where he had already been bitten. The line showed clearly on the top of his brown head and back where the brain joined the spinal cord and the old man drove the knife on the oar into the juncture, withdrew it, and drove it in again into the shark's yellow cat-like eyes. The shark let go of the fish and slid down, swallowing what he had taken as he died.

另一條鯊魚還在糟蹋大魚，弄得小船依然晃個不停。老人鬆開帆腳索，好讓小船往側面傾斜，露出船底的鯊魚來。他一見鯊魚便靠到船邊去刺它。他刺中的只是魚肉，魚皮死硬，刀子才勉強刺進去，卻震得他雙手和肩膀生疼。鯊魚飛快地浮上來，腦袋露出水面，老人趁鯊魚的鼻子出水倚著大魚的時候，對著它扁平腦袋的正中扎了下去。老人又拔出刀刃，對著同一個地方再次扎下去。鯊魚咬住大魚，嘴巴掛在大魚上。老人刺進它左眼，鯊魚卻依舊懸在那兒。

「這還不行嗎？」老人說，把刀刃刺進鯊魚脊椎和腦袋之間的地方。這一下很容易扎，而且他覺得鯊魚的軟骨斷了。老人將槳倒過來，把槳片塞進鯊魚嘴巴，要把它撬開。他旋轉了一下槳片，鯊魚鬆開了嘴巴，老人說：「別停下，加拉諾鯊，溜到底下一英里深的地方去吧。去見你的朋友，或者，見你媽去吧。」

The skiff was still shaking with the destruction the other shark was doing to the fish and the old man let go the sheet so that the skiff would swing broadside and bring the shark out from under. When he saw the shark he leaned over the side and punched at him. He hit only meat and the hide was set hard and he barely got the knife in. The blow hurt not only his hands but his shoulder too. But the shark came up fast with his head out and the old man hit him squarely in the center of his flat-topped head as his nose came out of water and lay against the fish. The old man withdrew the blade and punched the shark exactly in the same spot again. He still hung to the fish with his jaws hooked and the old man stabbed him in his left eye. The shark still hung there.

"No?" the old man said and he drove the blade between the vertebrae and the brain. It was an easy shot now and he felt the cartilage sever. The old man reversed the oar and put the blade between the shark's jaws to open them. He twisted the blade and as the shark slid loose he said, "Go on, *galano*. Slide down a mile deep. Go see your friend, or maybe it's your mother."

老人擦了擦刀刃，把槳放下了。隨後他找到了帆腳索，這時船帆已經鼓起，他把小船調整到原先的航道上。

「它們準已咬走了四分之一條魚，而且是最好的肉。」他大聲說，「但願這是一個夢，但願我從來沒有釣到它。魚呀，我為此感到抱歉，這把一切都搞砸了。」他停了下來，現在已不想再看那條魚。它流盡了血，又經海浪拍打，顏色看上去像鏡子銀白色的背襯，但身上的條紋依然很顯眼。

「我不該離岸那麼遠，魚，」他說，「你不該，我也不該。很抱歉，魚。」

好吧，他自言自語地說，瞧瞧刀上的捆索，看有沒有被割斷。然後保養好你的這雙手，因為還會有更多的鯊魚來。

「但願我有一塊磨刀石，」老人檢查了槳柄頭上的捆索後說，「我應該帶一塊磨刀石來。」你應該帶上很多東西，他想。但是你沒有帶，老頭兒。現在不是去想缺少什麼的時候，該想一想憑現有的東西你能做什麼。

The old man wiped the blade of his knife and laid down the oar. Then he found the sheet and the sail filled and he brought the skiff onto her course.

"They must have taken a quarter of him and of the best meat," he said aloud. "I wish it were a dream and that I had never hooked him. I'm sorry about it, fish. It makes everything wrong." He stopped and he did not want to look at the fish now. Drained of blood and awash he looked the colour of the silver backing of a mirror and his stripes still showed.

"I shouldn't have gone out so far, fish," he said. "Neither for you nor for me. I'm sorry, fish."

Now, he said to himself. Look to the lashing on the knife and see if it has been cut. Then get your hand in order because there still is more to come.

"I wish I had a stone for the knife," the old man said after he had checked the lashing on the oar butt. "I should have brought a stone." You should have brought many things, he thought. But you did not bring them, old man. Now is no time to think of what you do not have. Think of what you can do with what there is.

「你給了我很多忠告，」他大聲說，「我聽厭了。」

他把舵柄夾在胳膊下，小船向前行駛的時候，他把雙手浸在海水裡。

「天知道最後一條鯊魚叼走了多少魚肉，」他說，「但是現在小船輕多了。」他不願去想咬爛了的魚腹。他明白，鯊魚每猛烈撞擊一次，就是撕掉一塊肉。這條魚給所有的鯊魚在海裡留下了一條長長的血腥帶，足有公路那麼寬。

這條魚夠一個人吃一冬，他想。別往那兒想了。還是好好歇息，努力把雙手調養好，保住剩下的魚肉吧。比起水裡的氣味來，我手上的血腥味根本不算一回事，更何況出血又不多。割破的地方已無礙，左手出血還可以讓手不再抽筋。

"You give me much good counsel," he said aloud. "I'm tired of it."

He held the tiller under his arm and soaked both his hands in the water as the skiff drove forward.

"God knows how much that last one took," he said. "But she's much lighter now." He did not want to think of the mutilated under-side of the fish. He knew that each of the jerking bumps of the shark had been meat torn away and that the fish now made a trail for all sharks as wide as a highway through the sea.

He was a fish to keep a man all winter, he thought. Don't think of that. Just rest and try to get your hands in shape to defend what is left of him. The blood smell from my hands means nothing now with all that scent in the water. Besides they do not bleed much. There is nothing cut that means anything. The bleeding may keep the left from cramping.

現在我能想什麼呢？他想。沒有什麼是可以想的。我什麼也別想，光等後面的鯊魚來吧。但願這真的是一場夢，他想。但是誰知道呢？也許結局會很好。

接著趕到的是一條獨來獨往的六鰓鯊。要是豬有那麼大的嘴，讓你可以把頭伸進去，那麼這條鯊魚活像是一頭直奔食槽的豬。老人任它襲擊大魚，接著他把綁在槳上的刀往下一推，刺進了鯊魚的腦袋。不過鯊魚滾動著身子，往後急退，折斷了刀子。

老人靜下心來操舵。他甚至沒有去看大鯊魚慢慢地下沉，起初露出整個身子，後來變小了，後來成了一丁點。那情景常使老人著迷，但這一回，他連看都沒看。

「現在我還有那把手鉤，」他說，「但那東西沒有用。我有兩把槳，還有舵柄，還有短棍。」

What can I think of now? he thought. Nothing. I must think of nothing and wait for the next ones. I wish it had really been a dream, he thought. But who knows? It might have turned out well.

The next shark that came was a single shovelnose. He came like a pig to the trough if a pig had a mouth so wide that you could put your head in it. The old man let him hit the fish and then drove the knife on the oar down into his brain. But the shark jerked backwards as he rolled and the knife blade snapped.

The old man settled himself to steer. He did not even watch the big shark sinking slowly in the water, showing first life-size, then small, then tiny. That always fascinated the old man. But he did not even watch it now.

"I have the gaff now," he said. "But it will do no good. I have the two oars and the tiller and the short club."

現在它們把我擊敗了，他想。我太老了，沒法用棍子把鯊魚打死。但是，只要我還有槳，還有短棍，還有舵柄，我就要試一試。

他又把手浸到海水裡。這時已漸漸到了傍晚，除了大海和天空，什麼也看不到。空中的風比剛才要大。他希望不久會看到陸地。

「你累了，老頭子，」他說，「你的心累了。」

直到日落之前不久，鯊魚才又來攻擊。

老人看到幾根棕色的鰭，它們沿著準是大魚在水中留下的寬闊蹤跡追蹤過來，甚至沒有東聞西嗅尋找氣味，便直奔小船，並排游著。

他卡住了舵，繫好帆腳索，伸手到船尾下去拿棍子。這是一把斷槳的柄，鋸成了大約兩英寸半長。因為手柄很短，他只能用一隻手發力。他右手拿起短棍，緊緊握住，看著鯊魚過來。兩條都是加拉諾鯊。

Now they have beaten me, he thought. I am too old to club sharks to death. But I will try it as long as I have the oars and the short club and the tiller.

He put his hands in the water again to soak them. It was getting late in the afternoon and he saw nothing but the sea and the sky. There was more wind in the sky than there had been, and soon he hoped that he would see land.

"You're tired, old man," he said. "You're tired inside."

The sharks did not hit him again until just before sunset.

The old man saw the brown fins coming along the wide trail the fish must make in the water. They were not even quartering on the scent. They were headed straight for the skiff swimming side by side.

He jammed the tiller, made the sheet fast and reached under the stern for the club. It was an oar handle from a broken oar sawed off to about two and a half feet in length. He could only use it effectively with one hand because of the grip of the handle and he took good hold of it with his right hand, flexing his hand on it, as he watched the sharks come. They were both *galanos*.

「我得讓第一條鯊魚牢牢咬住了再動手打它的鼻尖，或者直接打它的頭頂。」他想。

兩條鯊魚同時逼近。他看見離他最近的一條張大嘴巴，咬住了大魚銀色的一側，於是便高高舉起短棍，重重地敲了下去，打在鯊魚大腦袋的頂上。短棍敲上去有一種敲在堅實的橡皮上的感覺。但是他也感覺到了僵硬的骨頭。鯊魚從大魚身上往下滑的時候，他又狠狠地敲打鯊魚的鼻尖。

另一條鯊魚在游進游出，這時張大了嘴又游了過來。鯊魚撞擊著大魚，咬緊了嘴巴，老人看到幾塊白花花的魚肉從它的嘴角掛下來。他向這條鯊魚打去，卻只敲在頭上。那鯊魚看著他，把肉叼走了。鯊魚溜走，把肉吞下的那一剎那，老人再次揮動短棍朝它打去，卻只擊在厚實的橡皮上。

「來吧，加拉諾鯊，」老人說，「再游過來吧。」

I must let the first one get a good hold and hit him on the point of the nose or straight across the top of the head, he thought.

The two sharks closed together and as he saw the one nearest him open his jaws and sink them into the silver side of the fish, he raised the club high and brought it down heavy and slamming onto the top of the shark's broad head. He felt the rubbery solidity as the club came down. But he felt the rigidity of bone too and he struck the shark once more hard across the point of the nose as he slid down from the fish.

The other shark had been in and out and now came in again with his jaws wide. The old man could see pieces of the meat of the fish spilling white from the corner of his jaws as he bumped the fish and closed his jaws. He swung at him and hit only the head and the shark looked at him and wrenched the meat loose. The old man swung the club down on him again as he slipped away to swallow and hit only the heavy solid rubberiness.

"Come on, *galano*," the old man said. "Come in again."

鯊魚急匆匆游過來了，正要合上嘴巴，老人就下手了，把短棍舉得不能再高，結結實實地打了它。這回他覺得打到了腦袋根部的骨頭。鯊魚無力地把肉叼走，從大魚身上滑下來的時候，老人又敲打了同一個地方。

老人提防鯊魚再來，但沒有一條再露面。隨後他看到一條在水面上打轉，卻沒有見到另外一條的鰭。

我不能指望把它們給宰了，他想。年輕時倒是可以。不過，我已讓它們倆都受了重傷，沒有一條會好過。要是我能用雙手擊棍，那肯定能把第一條宰了，甚至就是現在也行，他想。

他不想去看大魚，知道半條魚已經給咬爛了。他同鯊魚搏鬥時太陽已經下沉。

「天很快就會黑，」他說，「然後我該看到哈瓦那的燈光。要是我往東太遠了，我會看到其中一個新近開發的沙灘的燈光。」

The shark came in a rush and the old man hit him as he shut his jaws. He hit him solidly and from as high up as he could raise the club. This time he felt the bone at the base of the brain and he hit him again in the same place while the shark tore the meat loose sluggishly and slid down from the fish.

The old man watched for him to come again but neither shark showed. Then he saw one on the surface swimming in circles. He did not see the fin of the other.

I could not expect to kill them, he thought. I could have in my time. But I have hurt them both badly and neither one can feel very good. If I could have used a bat with two hands I could have killed the first one surely. Even now, he thought.

He did not want to look at the fish. He knew that half of him had been destroyed. The sun had gone down while he had been in the fight with the sharks.

"It will be dark soon," he said. "Then I should see the glow of Havana. If I am too far to the eastward I will see the lights of one of the new beaches."

現在我不可能離陸地太遠了。我希望沒有人會太擔心。當然只有那個男孩會擔心。但是，可以肯定他很有信心。很多年長一點的漁夫會擔心，很多其他人也會擔心，他想。我生活在一個很好的小鎮裡。

他沒法再跟魚說話了，因為它已經被咬得稀巴爛。隨後他想起了什麼。

「半條魚，」他說，「你原來是整條的。很遺憾我走得離岸太遠了。我把我們倆都毀了。不過我們還是宰了很多鯊魚，你和我，而且也毀了很多別的魚。你宰過多少魚，魚老？你頭上的矛不是白生的。」

他喜歡想這條魚，想它要是能自由游弋，會怎樣對付一條鯊魚。我應該砍下它的嘴巴，用它來跟鯊魚搏鬥，他想。可是沒有斧子，更沒有小刀。

但是，如果我有，而且能夠將魚嘴綁在槳柄上，那會是一件多好的武器！那樣我們就可以共同對付鯊魚了。要是它們晚上來，你怎麼辦呢？你能做什麼呢？

I cannot be too far out now, he thought. I hope no one has been too worried. There is only the boy to worry, of course. But I am sure he would have confidence. Many of the older fishermen will worry. Many others too, he thought. I live in a good town.

He could not talk to the fish anymore because the fish had been ruined too badly. Then something came into his head.

"Half fish," he said. "Fish that you were. I am sorry that I went too far out. I ruined us both. But we have killed many sharks, you and I, and ruined many others. How many did you ever kill, old fish? You do not have that spear on your head for nothing."

He liked to think of the fish and what he could do to a shark if he were swimming free. I should have chopped the bill off to fight them with, he thought. But there was no hatchet and then there was no knife.

But if I had, and could have lashed it to an oar butt, what a weapon. Then we might have fought them together. What will you do now if they come in the night? What can you do?

「同它們鬥，」他說，「我會一直鬥到死。」

但現在一片漆黑，不見光亮，也沒有燈光，只有風在颳，帆不住地拖扯著。他覺得說不定自己已經死了。他雙手併攏，碰了碰手掌。雙手並沒有死，只要一開一合，就能感到活生生地痛。他背靠船尾，知道自己並沒有死，這是肩膀的疼痛告訴他的。

我還有那些祈禱要做，要是捕到魚的話，我答應過要做的，他想。但是現在我累得做不動了。我還是把麻袋拿來披在肩上吧。

他躺在船尾，操著舵，等待天空出現亮光。我還有半條魚，他想。也許我走運，能把前半條帶回去。我得有點運氣。不，他說，你走得離岸太遠，這就毀了你的運氣。

「別傻了，」他大聲說，「別睡著了，掌你的舵。你可能還有不少運氣呢。」

"Fight them," he said. "I'll fight them until I die."

But in the dark now and no glow showing and no lights and only the wind and the steady pull of the sail he felt that perhaps he was already dead. He put his two hands together and felt the palms. They were not dead and he could bring the pain of life by simply opening and closing them. He leaned his back against the stern and knew he was not dead. His shoulders told him.

I have all those prayers I promised if I caught the fish, he thought. But I am too tired to say them now. I better get the sack and put it over my shoulders.

He lay in the stern and steered and watched for the glow to come in the sky. I have half of him, he thought. Maybe I'll have the luck to bring the forward half in. I should have some luck. No, he said. You violated your luck when you went too far outside.

"Don't be silly," he said aloud. "And keep awake and steer. You may have much luck yet."

「要是有地方出賣運氣，我倒願意買一些。」他說。

我用什麼來買呢？他問自己。難道用丟掉的魚叉、斷了的小刀，還有一雙壞手？

「也許你可以，」他說，「你在海上待了八十四天，想要拿它來買運氣。它們也差一點賣給你了。」

我決不能胡思亂想了，他想。運氣是以很多不同的形式出現的，誰能認出它來呢？不過我願意買一些，不管以什麼形式，不管要多少錢。但願我能看到燈火的亮光，他想。我希望得到的東西太多。但這是我現在希望得到的東西。他竭力把自己安頓得舒適些來操舵，而且他知道自己並沒有死，因為身上還在疼。

"I'd like to buy some if there's any place they sell it," he said.

What could I buy it with? he asked himself. Could I buy it with a lost harpoon and a broken knife and two bad hands?

"You might," he said. "You tried to buy it with eighty-four days at sea. They nearly sold it to you too."

I must not think nonsense, he thought. Luck is a thing that comes in many forms and who can recognize her? I would take some though in any form and pay what they asked. I wish I could see the glow from the lights, he thought. I wish too many things. But that is the thing I wish for now. He tried to settle more comfortably to steer and from his pain he knew he was not dead.

準是在夜裡十點左右，他看到了城市燈光的倒影。開始不過隱約可見，就像月亮升起前的天光。隨後，隔著隨風力加大而變得洶湧的海洋，這些光漸漸地清晰。他在光影中駕駛著，想必很快就會抵達海流的邊緣了。

現在事情已經過去了，他想。它們很可能會再來襲擊我。但是，一個人沒有武器，身在黑暗中，拿什麼來跟它們鬥呢？

現在他身子又僵又疼，他的傷口和身上所有用力的部位在夜晚的寒氣中痛得厲害。我希望不必再搏鬥了，他想。我多麼希望不必再搏鬥了。

但是到了半夜，他還是搏鬥了，這回他明白搏鬥是徒勞的。它們成群地游來，他只能看到它們的鰭在水中劃出一道道線，還有它們撲向大魚時留下的磷光。他用短棍去打鯊魚頭，聽見鯊魚嘴巴喀嚓咬下去，在底下咬住大魚時小船在搖晃。他只能憑感覺和聽覺死命打下去，只覺得短棍被什麼東西抓住，就沒了。

He saw the reflected glare of the lights of the city at what must have been around ten o'clock at night. They were only perceptible at first as the light is in the sky before the moon rises. Then they were steady to see across the ocean which was rough now with the increasing breeze. He steered inside of the glow and he thought that now, soon, he must hit the edge of the stream.

Now it is over, he thought. They will probably hit me again. But what can a man do against them in the dark without a weapon?

He was stiff and sore now and his wounds and all of the strained parts of his body hurt with the cold of the night. I hope I do not have to fight again, he thought. I hope so much I do not have to fight again.

But by midnight he fought and this time he knew the fight was useless. They came in a pack and he could only see the lines in the water that their fins made and their phosphorescence as they threw themselves on the fish. He clubbed at heads and heard the jaws chop and the shaking of the skiff as they took hold below. He clubbed desperately at what he could only feel and hear and he felt something seize the club and it was gone.

他猛地從船舵上拉下舵柄，用它亂打亂砍，雙手握住舵柄一次次猛砸下去。但是這時它們到了船頭，一個接著一個，或者成群地撲上來，把肉一塊塊地撕下。轉身再來時，這些肉在水下閃著光。

最後一條鯊魚向魚頭直撲過去，他知道這下完了。這時鯊魚的嘴被撕不下來的沉甸甸的魚頭卡住了，他用舵柄砸向鯊魚頭，一次、兩次，砸了又砸。他聽見舵柄斷了，便用斷柄刺向鯊魚。他覺出斷柄刺了進去，知道它很鋒利，於是又往裡刺。鯊魚鬆開嘴巴，打著滾游走了。那是鯊魚群中最晚來的一條，再也沒有東西可供它們吃的了。

這時老人差點連氣都透不過來，他覺得嘴裡的味道怪怪的，是一種銅臭味，甜甜的。他害怕了一陣子，不過那味道並不太重。

他往海裡吐了口痰，說：「你吃吧，加拉諾鯊。做個夢吧，夢見你殺了一個人。」

He jerked the tiller free from the rudder and beat and chopped with it, holding it in both hands and driving it down again and again. But they were up to the bow now and driving in one after the other and together, tearing off the pieces of meat that showed glowing below the sea as they turned to come once more.

One came, finally, against the head itself and he knew that it was over. He swung the tiller across the shark's head where the jaws were caught in the heaviness of the fish's head which would not tear. He swung it once and twice and again. He heard the tiller break and he lunged at the shark with the splintered butt. He felt it go in and knowing it was sharp he drove it in again. The shark let go and rolled away. That was the last shark of the pack that came. There was nothing more for them to eat.

The old man could hardly breathe now and he felt a strange taste in his mouth. It was coppery and sweet and he was afraid of it for a moment. But there was not much of it.

He spat into the ocean and said, "Eat that, *Galanos*. And make a dream you've killed a man."

他知道自己終於被擊垮了，而且無法進行任何補救。他回到船尾，發現儘管舵柄的一頭已經參差不齊，但還是能塞進舵孔，讓他多少可以駕駛。他把麻袋披在肩上，駕著小船上路了。他輕鬆地駕著船，沒有任何想法和感覺。他現在已經超脫一切，只是盡心盡力地駕著小船朝目的港駛去。夜裡鯊魚襲擊了魚骨，就像人從桌上撿起麵包屑那樣。老人不去理它們，除了駕駛，他什麼也不在意。現在他只注意到，沒有了船邊的重物，小船行駛起來那麼輕巧、那麼順暢。

這船不錯，他想。除了舵柄，它完好無損，而舵柄是很容易更換的。

他能感覺到小船已駛進海流，看得見岸上沙灘村落的燈光了。他知道現在他已經到了哪裡，回家已毫不費力。

He knew he was beaten now finally and without remedy and he went back to the stern and found the jagged end of the tiller would fit in the slot of the rudder well enough for him to steer. He settled the sack around his shoulders and put the skiff on her course. He sailed lightly now and he had no thoughts nor any feelings of any kind. He was past everything now and he sailed the skiff to make his home port as well and as intelligently as he could. In the night sharks hit the carcass as someone might pick up crumbs from the table. The old man paid no attention to them and did not pay any attention to anything except steering. He only noticed how lightly and how well the skiff sailed now there was no great weight beside her.

She's good, he thought. She is sound and not harmed in any way except for the tiller. That is easily replaced.

He could feel he was inside the current now and he could see the lights of the beach colonies along the shore. He knew where he was now and it was nothing to get home.

無論如何，風是我們的朋友，他想。隨後他補充道，有時候是。還有大海，海裡有我們的朋友和敵人。還有床，他想。床是我的朋友。就只是床，他想。床是一件了不起的東西。被打垮倒反而輕鬆了，他想。我從來不知道會這麼輕鬆。是什麼把你擊垮的呢？他想。

「什麼也沒有，」他大聲說，「我出海太遠了。」

他駛進小港的時候，露臺飯館屋頂上的燈滅了，他知道大家都已上床。海風愈颳愈大，這時已十分強勁，但是海港十分寧靜。他駛進了岩石下的一小片砂石灘，沒有人幫忙，他便獨自把船往上划，離海盡量遠些。隨後他跨出船，把小船繫在一塊岩石上。

The wind is our friend, anyway, he thought. Then he added, sometimes. And the great sea with our friends and our enemies. And bed, he thought. Bed is my friend. Just bed, he thought. Bed will be a great thing. It is easy when you are beaten, he thought. I never knew how easy it was. And what beat you, he thought.

"Nothing," he said aloud. "I went out too far."

When he sailed into the little harbour the lights of the Terrace were out and he knew everyone was in bed. The breeze had risen steadily and was blowing strongly now. It was quiet in the harbour though and he sailed up onto the little patch of shingle below the rocks. There was no one to help him so he pulled the boat up as far as he could. Then he stepped out and made her fast to a rock.

他取下桅杆，捲起船帆，把它捆好。接著他扛起桅杆，開始往上爬，這時候他才知道自己有多累。他停了一會兒，回頭瞧了瞧，在水裡街燈的倒影中，看到了巨大的魚尾，直豎著，好長一段拖在船尾後面。他看到了背脊裸露的白線，黑乎乎的魚頭，伸出的長嘴，頭尾之間光禿禿的沒有一點肉。

他又開始往上爬，到了頂上摔倒了，他躺了一會兒，桅杆斜壓在肩上。他掙扎著要起來，但太難了。他扛著桅杆坐在那兒，朝路那邊望去。一隻貓從路對面經過，忙著自己的事兒。老人看著它。然後他只是瞧著路。

最後他放下桅杆，站了起來。他又拿起桅杆，放在肩上，開始往上走，坐下來歇了五次才走回自己的小棚屋。

He unstepped the mast and furled the sail and tied it. Then he shouldered the mast and started to climb. It was then he knew the depth of his tiredness. He stopped for a moment and looked back and saw in the reflection from the street light the great tail of the fish standing up well behind the skiff's stern. He saw the white naked line of his backbone and the dark mass of the head with the projecting bill and all the nakedness between.

He started to climb again and at the top he fell and lay for some time with the mast across his shoulder. He tried to get up. But it was too difficult and he sat there with the mast on his shoulder and looked at the road. A cat passed on the far side going about its business and the old man watched it. Then he just watched the road.

Finally he put the mast down and stood up. He picked the mast up and put it on his shoulder and started up the road. He had to sit down five times before he reached his shack.

在棚屋裡，他把桅杆豎在牆邊，摸黑找到了一個水瓶，喝了口水。隨後他在床上躺了下來。他把毯子拉過來蓋在肩上，然後蓋在背上和腿上，他臉朝下趴在報紙上，胳膊伸直，掌心朝上。

早上那孩子從門外探進頭來時，他正在熟睡。風颳得太厲害，漂浮著的船隻不會出海。孩子睡得很晚，而且跟每天早晨一樣，他來到老人的棚屋。孩子看見老人在呼吸，隨後又看到了他的手，於是便哭了起來。他悄悄地出門去弄些咖啡，一路上都在哭著。

很多漁夫圍在船邊，看著綁在船沿上的東西。其中的一個捲起了褲腿站在水裡，用一段繩子在丈量魚的骨架。

孩子沒有下去，他已經去過那裡。一個漁夫在為他看管小船。

「他怎麼樣？」一個漁夫叫道。

Inside the shack he leaned the mast against the wall. In the dark he found a water bottle and took a drink. Then he lay down on the bed. He pulled the blanket over his shoulders and then over his back and legs and he slept face down on the newspapers with his arms out straight and the palms of his hands up.

He was asleep when the boy looked in the door in the morning. It was blowing so hard that the drifting-boats would not be going out and the boy had slept late and then come to the old man's shack as he had come each morning. The boy saw that the old man was breathing and then he saw the old man's hands and he started to cry. He went out very quietly to go to bring some coffee and all the way down the road he was crying.

Many fishermen were around the skiff looking at what was lashed beside it and one was in the water, his trousers rolled up, measuring the skeleton with a length of line.

The boy did not go down. He had been there before and one of the fishermen was looking after the skiff for him.

"How is he?" one of the fishermen shouted.

「在睡覺呢。」孩子叫道。他不在乎人家看見他在哭，「誰也別去打攪他。」

「從鼻子到尾巴有十八英尺長。」正在丈量的漁夫叫道。

「我相信。」孩子說。

他走進露臺飯館，要了一罐咖啡。

「要熱的，多加些牛奶和糖。」

「還要別的嗎？」

「不要了，等會兒我看他能吃些什麼。」

「多好的魚呀，」老闆說，「從來沒有見過這樣的魚。你昨天捕到的兩條也是好魚。」

「讓我的魚見鬼去吧。」孩子說著又哭了起來。

"Sleeping," the boy called. He did not care that they saw him crying. "Let no one disturb him."

"He was eighteen feet from nose to tail," the fisherman who was measuring him called.

"I believe it," the boy said.

He went into the Terrace and asked for a can of coffee.

"Hot and with plenty of milk and sugar in it."

"Anything more?"

"No. Afterwards I will see what he can eat."

"What a fish it was," the proprietor said. "There has never been such a fish. Those were two fine fish you took yesterday too."

"Damn my fish," the boy said and he started to cry again.

「你要什麼飲料嗎？」老闆問。

「不要，」孩子說，「告訴他們別打攪聖地牙哥。我會回來的。」

「告訴他我心裡有多難過。」

「謝謝。」孩子說。

孩子拎了一罐熱咖啡，走到了老人的棚屋，坐在他旁邊，直到老人醒過來。有一回他看上去像是醒來了，但是又沉沉地睡了過去。孩子穿過馬路，借些木頭來熱咖啡。

老人終於醒來了。

「別坐起來，」孩子說，「喝點這個。」他往杯子裡倒了些咖啡。

老人接過咖啡，喝了下去。

「它們打垮了我，曼諾林，」他說，「它們確實打垮了我。」

"Do you want a drink of any kind?" the proprietor asked.

"No," the boy said. "Tell them not to bother Santiago. I'll be back."

"Tell him how sorry I am."

"Thanks," the boy said.

The boy carried the hot can of coffee up to the old man's shack and sat by him until he woke. Once it looked as though he were waking. But he had gone back into heavy sleep and the boy had gone across the road to borrow some wood to heat the coffee.

Finally the old man woke.

"Don't sit up," the boy said. "Drink this." He poured some of the coffee in a glass.

The old man took it and drank it.

"They beat me, Manolin," he said. "They truly beat me."

「它沒有打垮你，那條魚沒有打垮你。」

「是啊，那倒是。是後來的事。」

「佩德里科照看著小船和漁具。你打算拿魚頭怎麼辦？」

「讓佩德里科把它切碎做誘餌吧。」

「還有尖尖的魚嘴呢？」

「你要就留著吧。」

「我要，」孩子說，「現在我們得計畫一下其他的事情了。」

「他們找過我嗎？」

「當然，動用了海岸警衛隊和飛機。」

"He didn't beat you. Not the fish."

"No. Truly. It was afterwards."

"Pedrico is looking after the skiff and the gear. What do you want done with the head?"

"Let Pedrico chop it up to use in fish traps."

"And the spear?"

"You keep it if you want it."

"I want it," the boy said. "Now we must make our plans about the other things."

"Did they search for me?"

"Of course. With coast guard and with planes."

「海洋那麼大，船又那麼小，很難看得到。」老人說。他注意到，有人可以交談，而不是自言自語和對著大海說話，是件多麼愉快的事兒。「我想著你呢，」他說，「你捕到什麼啦？」

「第一天一條，第二天一條，第三天兩條。」

「很好啊。」

「現在我們又可以一起捕魚了。」

「不，我的運氣不好。我再也不會走運了。」

「讓運氣見鬼去吧，」孩子說，「我會帶來運氣。」

「你家裡人會怎麼說？」

「我不在乎。昨天我捉到了兩條。但現在我們要一起捕魚了，我需要學的還很多。」

"The ocean is very big and a skiff is small and hard to see," the old man said. He noticed how pleasant it was to have someone to talk to instead of speaking only to himself and to the sea. "I missed you," he said. "What did you catch?"

"One the first day. One the second and two the third."

"Very good."

"Now we fish together again."

"No. I am not lucky. I am not lucky anymore."

"The hell with luck," the boy said. "I'll bring the luck with me."

"What will your family say?"

"I do not care. I caught two yesterday. But we will fish together now for I still have much to learn."

「我們得搞一支很好的魚鏢，一直在船上備著。你可以用舊福特車上的彈簧片做刀刃。可以拿到瓜納瓦科阿去打磨。這樣應該會很鋒利，不要回火，免得把它弄斷。我的刀就斷了。」

「我再搞一把刀，把彈簧磨好。這大風要颳多少天？」

「可能三天。也可能更長一點。」

「我把一切都準備好，」孩子說，「你把你的手養好，老爺子。」

「我知道怎麼保養。夜裡，我吐出了一些奇怪的東西，覺得胸膛裡什麼東西壞了。」

「把那也養好，」孩子說，「躺下，老爺子，我會把你的乾淨襯衫送來，還有一些吃的。」

「我不在的那些日子的報紙，也拿一份來。」老人說。

"We must get a good killing lance and always have it on board. You can make the blade from a spring leaf from an old Ford. We can grind it in Guanabacoa. It should be sharp and not tempered so it will break. My knife broke."

"I'll get another knife and have the spring ground. How many days of heavy brisa have we?"

"Maybe three. Maybe more."

"I will have everything in order," the boy said. "You get your hands well old man."

"I know how to care for them. In the night I spat something strange and felt something in my chest was broken."

"Get that well too," the boy said. "Lie down, old man, and I will bring you your clean shirt. And something to eat."

"Bring any of the papers of the time that I was gone," the old man said.

「你得盡快養好，我有那麼多東西要學，而你什麼都能教。你受了多少苦呀？」

「很多。」老人說。

「我會送吃的和報紙過來。」孩子說，「好好休息，老爺子。我會從藥店給你搞些治手的藥來。」

「別忘了告訴佩德里科，魚頭歸他了。」

「不會忘記的，我記著呢。」

孩子出了門，沿著破損的珊瑚石路走著，又哭了起來。

那天下午，露臺飯館裡來了一群遊客，其中一個女的往下瞧著海水，在空啤酒罐和死梭魚中間，看到了一根又大又長的白色脊柱骨，骨頭的末端聳立著一個巨大的尾巴。東風在港口不斷掀起大浪的時候，尾巴隨著波濤起伏。

"You must get well fast for there is much that I can learn and you can teach me everything. How much did you suffer?"

"Plenty," the old man said.

"I'll bring the food and the papers," the boy said. "Rest well, old man. I will bring stuff from the drugstore for your hands."

"Don't forget to tell Pedrico the head is his."

"No. I will remember."

As the boy went out the door and down the worn coral rock road he was crying again.

That afternoon there was a party of tourists at the Terrace and looking down in the water among the empty beer cans and dead barracudas a woman saw a great long white spine with a huge tail at the end that lifted and swung with the tide while the east wind blew a heavy steady sea outside the entrance to the harbour.

「那是什麼？」她指著大魚長長的背脊骨問一個侍者，現在背脊只不過是一堆垃圾，等著被潮水沖走。

「Tiburon[22]，」侍者說，「Eshark[23]。」他正打算解釋一下事情的來龍去脈。

「我以前可不知道鯊魚有這麼漂亮、樣子這麼好看的尾巴。」

「我也不知道。」她的一個男旅伴說。

在路另一頭的棚屋裡，老人又睡著了。他還是臉朝下睡著，而那個孩子就坐在他旁邊，看著他。老人正夢見獅子。

22 西班牙語，意為「鯊魚」。

23 侍者用英語表達「鯊魚」時的不正確發音。

"What's that?" she asked a waiter and pointed to the long backbone of the great fish that was now just garbage waiting to go out with the tide.

"*Tiburon*," the waiter said. "Eshark." He was meaning to explain what had happened.

"I didn't know sharks had such handsome, beautifully formed tails."

"I didn't either," her male companion said.

Up the road, in his shack, the old man was sleeping again. He was still sleeping on his face and the boy was sitting by him watching him. The old man was dreaming about the lions.

必讀經典 : 老人與海/海明威(Ernet
Hemingway)著 ; 黃源深譯. -- 初版. -- 新竹市
: 大溏文化事業有限公司出版 : 大和書報圖書
股份有限公司發行, 2024.12, 2024.09
面； 公分
中英對照
譯自 : The old man and the sea.
ISBN 978-626-98924-4-0(平裝)

874.57 113017351

**必讀經典：老人與海【中英對照典藏版・權威教授譯本】**

The Old Man and the Sea

作者 海明威（Ernest Hemingway）
特約編輯・排版 張立雯
封面設計・內頁插圖 Dinner Illustration
行銷部 蔡幃誠
發行人兼出版總監 蔡建志
出版 大溏文化事業有限公司
發行 大和書報圖書股份有限公司
地址 新竹市工業東二路11號
電話 0927697870

印刷 呈靖彩藝有限公司
初版 2024年12月 定價 350元
初版三刷 2025年10月